MIDNIGHT OBSESSION

SOULMATED
BOOK 5

REBECCA YORK

With an angry curse, Harold Goddard slammed his fist against his desk, making the bottles on the nearby liquor cart rattle. He winced as the shock of the powerful blow reverberated up his arm.

The clacking bottles drew his attention. Standing, he crossed to the cart, snatched up a highball glass, and poured himself two fingers of Jack Daniels. After downing the first swallow in a gulp, he warned himself to slow down. He had to keep a clear head if he was going to get out of this mess.

He ran a shaky hand through his thinning, salt-and-pepper hair. Okay, he silently admitted, he had killed the wrong man. But his plan should have been foolproof. No more trying to capture a pair of the devil's spawn from that nutball Louisiana fertility clinic. Down in Mardi Gras country when they were under threat, some sixth sense had them teaming up with other couples of their kind.

Since that group dynamic made them even more dangerous, he'd decided to do his hunting in a safer environment where any individual would naturally be more isolated. And no more thoughts of experimenting to find out what a mated pair could do together. That was simply too risky, because when they hooked up, they were more than the sum of their parts.

Capturing only one was safer. He'd settle for an intense interrogation before getting rid of the evidence. That should be enough.

He'd found the perfect candidate. A loner, like a lot of the people born from those fertility clinic experiments. A guy whose body would be easy to dispose of because his job took him away from home base on a regular basis. Someone who would jump at the chance to earn a tempting fee for a few days' easy work. The plan was genius.

Except that it turned out it wasn't. A detective from some hotshot private agency called Decorah Security was poking into the guy's death. And it looked like Harold was going to have to eliminate *him*, too. Then what? Would he have to go up against another agent from the company? Then another? Or would he have to blow up the whole place? He brought the glass of whiskey to his mouth again. First things first. Deal with the detective and adjust as needed.

OLIVIA LANGSTON WANTED TO SCREAM, but somehow her vocal cords wouldn't work. She knew she was having a nightmare—and one like no other she had ever experienced.

She couldn't utter a sound because the terrible dream was happening to someone else. She wasn't in her own body, in her own mind. She was another person. A man she didn't know. A man she had never met. Yet somehow she had been pulled into his reality.

His nightmare? Or was it actually real life? His life.

Rough hands seized him, pulled him to his feet, and dragged him across a cold floor. He tried to struggle, but his muscles wouldn't work. Maybe he'd been drugged.

A gruff voice was speaking, giving orders to his captors, and she strained to catch the words.

"Make sure he's alive when he goes into the water. If the body ever turns up, I want it clear that he drowned."

Desperately, Olivia tried to wrench herself away even as she knew they weren't talking about her. While she fought for understanding, she struggled to regain her sense of self. But breaking free was impossible. Getting back into the mind of Olivia Langston was as far beyond her as it would be to fly to the moon.

She was stuck in the consciousness of some unknown man—just as he was plunged into what must be the most horrible episode of his life. They picked him up, tossed him onto a hard surface, his head colliding with cold metal. Was he in the back of a pickup truck? He caught a glimpse of the night sky filled with stars before someone tossed a blanket over him. Then he felt motion as the vehicle started up and lurched forward.

After the endless ride, he was carried somewhere else—across wooden boards to a surface that rocked under him as the sound of waves reached his ears. They were on the water, in a boat, the rocking of the craft a familiar sensation.

His boat? Yes, he thought so. Memories came back to him. The joy of plowing through a sea smooth as glass as the red ball of the setting sun sank from view. The pleasure of landing an enormous fish that had given him a valiant fight. And then the terror of holding a course while fifteen-foot-high waves crashed over the deck. The calm after the storm, and the satisfaction of knowing he had brought his vessel through the tempest. All that and more flashed through his mind as the familiar rocking lulled him.

But safety was only an illusion. All too soon, the engine slowed. Then the captors' hands were on him again, pulling him from the cocoon of the blankets they had wrapped around him before they'd carried him from the truck across a dock and onto the boat.

Confusion threatened to swamp him. This couldn't be happening. But the scene was all too real.

They hoisted him by the arms and legs, swinging him in a great arc before they let go. He flew through the air, then plummeted into the water with a tremendous splash. As he sank into the cold darkness, he desperately tried to fight to the surface, but his muscles still didn't work. He tried to hold his breath, but it finally became impossible. When he gasped for air, water flooded his lungs.

His last sensations were terror, followed by resignation that there was no way out of this trap.

Olivia sat bolt upright in bed. Shuddering, she dragged blessed air into her lungs. Her heart was pounding so hard that she thought it would be visible through the wall of her chest.

Lord, where had that terrible dream come from? Nothing like that had ever happened to her before.

She focused on her breathing, willing herself back to calm. She was herself again. She was safe. It wasn't her.

It was that poor man. Thugs had murdered him, and she didn't even know why. It had been so real that she could believe it was true. For a fleeting moment, she thought she should call the police.

She shoved that thought out of her mind as quickly as it had arrived. If she made the call, she'd sound crazy. That last word hung in her mind.

Looking around, she confirmed that she was safe in her own room. She hadn't been in a boat. She hadn't been thrown overboard to die.

Again she told herself—it wasn't you. It was a man. And the whole thing had been as strange as it was terrifying. When had she ever experienced a dream from the point of view of another person—much less a man?

She shuddered. She had come in at the end of the guy's life. It seemed like he'd been held captive and maybe tortured before they'd dragged him to a boat and tossed him overboard like a sack of garbage.

Trying to banish the disturbing images, she pressed the heels of her hands against her eyes, but it did no good. The experience was burned into her brain. Where had it come from? Certainly not her own memory. She'd had some horrendous experiences in her life, but nothing like *this*.

She glanced at the clock. It was only four-thirty in the morning, but she knew she wasn't going back to sleep.

Swinging her legs out of bed, she stood unsteadily for several moments before scuffing on her slippers. She was wearing a T-shirt and yoga pants, her favorite sleeping outfit. If someone happened to ring the doorbell before she was ready to start the day, it looked like she was dressed.

She padded downstairs to the first floor of the big house she'd inherited from her parents. In the kitchen, she contemplated her collection of teas and selected a cranberry-orange blend. Dunking the bag into a mug of hot water, she set it in the microwave.

While she waited with her hips propped against a caramel-colored granite counter, she looked around the large room. Her mother would have said the kitchen needed updating, but she liked it this way, and Mom and Dad were no longer around to make her life a living hell— in their well-meaning way, of course. On a trip down to their vacation home near Asheville, a sudden fog had come up, and Dad had crashed his Cessna into a mountain.

It might be hard to understand that someone could feel relieved that her parents had left her an orphan at the tender age of twenty. But that was the main emotion she felt when she thought of them.

Long ago, she'd pushed all the old, whispered conversations between her parents out of her mind. Somehow the dream, or perhaps the aftermath, brought them zinging back.

"What's wrong with that child?...not normal...going to end up in a mental institution."

They'd dragged her to a series of psychiatrists and psychologists. She'd heard words like "on the spectrum, personality disorder, and latent schizophrenia." Later, out of what she considered morbid curiosity, she'd done some reading on her own and knew that full-blown mental illness might not burst forth until young adulthood. That worry had lingered in the back of her mind, but she'd always been able to tell herself that she was doing just fine on her own.

Olivia grabbed her mug out of the microwave and threw the tea bag in the trash. Mom would have saved it in a saucer on the counter to make another cup. Olivia had always hated the weak second brewing.

With the hot drink in hand, she wandered out to the sunroom. In her parents' day, it had been a screened porch, but she had enclosed it with big windows and added a heat pump to make it an all-year-round room. The furnishings were classic white wicker chairs with comfortable cushions, a wrought iron table, and a few of the painted furniture pieces she made her living selling. Pots of orchids and other flowering plants sat on the table and long benches under the windows. And she'd even brought in a couple of tall Ficus trees to give the room a tropical look.

This was her favorite spot in the house, and she settled into a comfortable chair, putting her mug on the nearby table.

The familiar setting soothed her, and she eased back in her chair, turning her attention to a more welcome topic—ideas for her next projects. She was almost finished painting whimsical cats on a chest of drawers. Next, it might be interesting to put colorful birds on a wooden tea cart.

As the new design took shape in her mind, she could almost convince herself that the dream had been nothing to worry about.

Almost.

CHAPTER TWO

Several days passed, and Olivia stopped worrying about the nightmare as she plunged back into the busy work schedule she'd set for herself. She had the vague feeling that something had disturbed the fabric of her life, but she didn't know what it was. And she could put it out of her mind for long stretches of time.

The house she'd inherited was in a rural area, but close enough to Frederick, Maryland, for her to have launched her career in the town. Although more than 270 years old, it had never grown like either nearby Baltimore or Washington. But in the 21st century, its antique, old-world charm was giving it a second life. Filled with specialty shops, restaurants, breweries, and art galleries, it had come into its own.

Olivia had gambled that her hand-painted furniture would be a perfect addition to some of the kitschy little shops. Her parents had insisted that she get a college degree in case what they referred to as *her self-indulgent artsy-fartsy plans* blew up in her face. After the plane crash, in an act of pure rebellion, she'd dropped out of Penn State and plunged into the life she'd always craved. With her inheritance as a cushion, she'd started from ground zero and made herself into a sought-after regional artist who turned junky old pieces of furniture and cheap raw wood chests, tables, chairs, and benches into beautifully designed masterpieces, decorated with all manner of witty designs.

It was a career she loved. She felt contented and fulfilled—or at least as contented and fulfilled as she could be.

Except in one area—real intimacy with another human being.

She flashed on a guy—Phil Hammond—the manager at Just for You, one of the shops downtown that carried her furniture. He was cute, and he obviously wanted to get to know her better. He'd asked her out a couple of times, and she'd always declined. She knew they might enjoy each other's company for a while, but from past experience, she understood it would only be on a superficial level. She might even find sleeping with him pleasant. But the relationship couldn't go any deeper. She just wasn't built for making a meaningful connection. Either she'd end up telling him things just weren't working out, or he'd realize on his own and look for someone else.

After showering and dressing, she wanted to head for her studio, but she knew she had been putting off the accounting tasks that were part of running a small business. If she didn't want to end up with late charges on her credit cards, she'd better pay some bills. And she should also check her spreadsheets to make sure she was bringing in the income she expected.

It was late morning before she strode down the brick walkway that meandered through the gardens she'd designed. They featured a cheerful mixture of annuals and perennials so that something was always blooming from snowdrops in mid-March to the last of the tall phlox in October.

Her studio was at the end of the walkway, the perfect location for an artist who needed to be alone with her work for long periods of time. The five-acre property she'd inherited came complete with a detached old carriage house. Her parents had used it as a garage. She had converted the building into a studio and parked her van in the driveway.

The only things she'd added were large windows that let in natural light and a small heat pump for climate control.

Inside, she began to add a few finishing touches to the chest of drawers a DC couple with a Capitol Hill townhouse had commissioned for their daughter's room. They'd seen her work in the dining room of a friend and decided they must have their own Olivia Langston original.

The background of the piece was a soft cream color, which she had decorated with whimsical cats in various poses, some playing with a variety of toys, some lying down, and one stunning tabby chasing its own tail. She was almost finished with the project. After it dried, she would arrange for delivery. And meanwhile, she could start on the tea cart.

Smiling, she stepped back and gave the chest a critical inspection. These cute felines were one of her better designs, if she did say so herself. The smile froze, and a sudden chill rippled over her skin. All at once, she knew she wasn't alone in her workshop.

Quickly, she whirled, staring at the space behind her. It was empty. Well, except for two lines of chairs, tables, chests, and a few other pieces. The front row was finished and ready for delivery to retail outlets. The back row was unpainted wood, ready for her attention.

They all stood exactly where they had been the day before. Yet she couldn't stop herself from putting down her brush, walking to the front row of furniture, and looking behind the larger pieces—seeing nothing.

Shaking her head, she turned back to the cats. But her next words were for the phantom watcher. In a voice that shook only slightly, she asked, "Well, what do you think? Are the Clarks going to love it?"

She waited for several pounding heartbeats to hear an answer. Of course, nobody responded, and she told herself she was being ridiculous. The invisible man wasn't in her workshop.

Grimacing, she covered the pallet of acrylic paints she'd been using and brought her brushes to the sink, where she carefully washed and dried them before cleaning the paint off her hands. Although she was determined to ignore the feeling of being watched, she couldn't shake it. Someone else was here. She knew it. Yet that was impossible.

Finally, as she took off her smock, anger mixed with fear burst through her determination.

First, that damn dream, and now this paranoid feeling that someone was watching her. Were her parents right? Was she destined to come unglued?

Her jaw set defiantly, she struggled to bring herself back on an even keel. But she knew she was too wound up to get any work done.

Because her mind and emotions were churning as she hurried back toward the kitchen door, she wasn't paying attention to the parts of the walk that needed attention. As she came even with the side of the house, her foot caught on a loose brick, and she pitched forward. With nothing to stop her fall, she was going to end up sprawled in one of the flower beds. Only it didn't happen.

As she sailed toward the ground, something caught her. No. Not some force of nature. A man. She was sure he had been watching her work. Then he had followed her from the studio, staying close behind her. When he saw her trip, he caught her in his strong arms.

Impossible. There was no one else here. But in that startling moment of not crashing to the ground, it was the only explanation.

With the realization, she felt everything change.

Deep down, she had admitted to herself that she was destined to be a solitary traveler through life, unable to make a lasting, meaningful connection to any other person. Now, as strange as it sounded, she sensed some kind of link forming with the man holding her in his arms.

She wasn't sure how she recognized it, but she felt a startling sense of completeness. And as it washed over her and sank into her bones, she recognized it for what it was. The thing she had always secretly craved. In that moment of awareness, she closed her eyes and leaned back, enjoying sensations that were new to her. Her senses swam, and at the same time, she was enveloped by something she had never experienced before—the comforting feeling of being cherished and protected.

Somewhere below those extraordinary feelings, she felt a headache pounding inside her skull. Ignoring it, she tipped her head back, using his muscular shoulder for a pillow. Although her eyes were squeezed shut, an image of him came into her mind, clear and distinct. She saw a tall man with angular features and high cheekbones. His dark hair was wind-tossed, his lips were firm, and his chin was a bold statement. His body was lean and supple. She felt hard muscles and sinew, honed from long hours working outside. This man was no desk jockey. When he tipped his head, she felt his breath teasing her ear. She had never liked to be touched. Now she craved it. For long moments, she drifted there, more content than she had ever been in her life. This was something totally different for her, yet she recognized it. This was what she had always assumed she could never have.

Wanting more, she dragged in a deep breath and

caught the strong smell of the sea. And as that scent came to her, she startled because it brought back the frightening dream she had struggled so hard to wipe out of her mind.

She gasped, horror gripping her by the throat as reality slammed into her little fantasy of being loved and cherished. Oh lord, this couldn't be real. What was happening now had to be impossible. Her damaged brain must be making it all up. Yet it took an act of will to shake the feeling that she had come home to the one thing in life she craved most.

Again, the word *impossible* rang in her mind. Moments ago, she had been alone on the brick walkway, fleeing some imaginary intruder in her studio. And, far from imaginary, he had followed her up the path.

No, that had to be wrong. No one else had been there. No one else was here now. Whatever was happening must be proof that her parents had been right all along.

Terror welled up from the depths of her soul—terror for her hold on sanity.

"Let me go," she gasped. She must break away. She must ground herself in facts—not a fantasy she had conjured from the depths of a damaged psyche.

Without waiting for him to comply, she tried to pull away.

He was strong. For long seconds, he held on to her with a kind of desperation, as though he couldn't bear to break the contact. As though nothing was real except the two of them joined here in a phantom embrace.

"Stop! Let me go," she said again, putting as much force as she could into the words.

The moment she felt his grip loosen, she wrenched herself away, almost falling again. It took several steps to regain her balance before she was sprinting headlong toward the house.

Reaching the kitchen door, she pulled it open, threw herself inside, and turned to shoot the deadbolt. With the barrier between herself and whatever was out of there, she stood shaking, unable to account for what had happened over the last few minutes. Had it been a waking dream? A psychotic break?

Her heart was pounding. Her breath was coming in gasps. Afraid that she might faint, she crossed to the table on shaky legs, pulled out a chair, and plopped onto the wooden seat.

My God, what had happened to her? Once again, the only explanation that came to mind was the madness her parents had predicted.

Turning, she looked out the window beside the door. Was she hoping to see a man standing there? Proof that she hadn't made up the whole incident? Of course, nobody was there. Nobody was making a tempting offer to fulfill the secret desire that she had barely been able to admit to herself.

Unable to sit still, she jumped up again and paced back and forth across the kitchen. Over the years, she'd done a lot of reading about mental illness. One book she'd picked up was *I Never Promised You a Rose Garden*. It was about a teenager who had descended into the clutches of schizo-phrenia. At first, the imaginary people who came to her were welcoming. Gradually, they turned hostile and controlling, making her life a living hell. That book had taught her that if she ever found herself in the same situation as that girl, she must resist the seduction of the false friends.

She knew she must do that now.

CHAPTER THREE

Olivia's legs turned wobbly, and she had to sit down again. Closing her eyes, she lowered her head to her arms as they rested on the table. It was happening—she was losing her mind. What else could this be? Should she call a doctor? Or maybe drive up to the nearest mental institution and check herself in, the way that girl in the book had? Or what if there was another explanation? What if something strange really was happening to her?

It had started with her nightmare where she witnessed the death of a man who was tossed off his own boat. Somehow, seeing his death had established a link between them. And now he had come to her home to haunt her.

Oh sure. Perfectly logical. Yet she couldn't stop wild thoughts from circling in her mind. The only good thing was that the headache she'd experienced out on the walk seemed to have evaporated.

Her lips firmed. She couldn't just sit here with her

head on her arms. And she couldn't leave her workshop unlocked. She had too many valuable pieces in there for her to leave them unprotected.

Finally, she stood up, straightened her shoulders, and turned toward the door. With her teeth gritted, she forced herself to step outside and march down the walk, watching her step so that she didn't trip again. It was tempting to look around, but she kept her gaze down. She hadn't seen anything before. Why would she see anything now? Still, she couldn't banish the feeling of something closing in around her.

She'd had a keyless entry mechanism installed on the workshop door. All she had to do was run her hand down the electronic pad until a little picture of a lock appeared. When she saw it, she pressed the icon, and the device clicked. As soon as the door was locked, she headed back to the house—to the sunroom.

She should be working, of course. She had the chest to finish and scores of orders to fill. And she wanted to sketch out the design for the tea cart. But she knew that anything she did would not be her best. How could she hold a pencil or her paintbrush steady when her hand was shaking?

No, work was out of the question. But she couldn't simply sit in the sunroom—her mind circling round and round like a dog finding a comfortable spot to settle.

Glancing at the clock, she saw it was well after lunchtime, but the idea of trying to choke anything down made her stomach roil.

No, she had to find something else to do. But what?

She had promised herself that she would organize all the stuff in the mudroom closet. Tackling it now would settle her.

Throwing open the closet door, she stood with her hands on her hips, looking at all the stuff she had tossed there to be sorted later. With a jerky motion, she pulled out a pair of boots and set them aside. They hadn't felt comfortable in years. She might as well pitch them.

After retrieving a couple of large plastic garbage bags, she began sorting items—those she wanted to put back into the closet and those that would go to an organization that regularly sent out trucks for donations.

While she worked, she found a song running through her head. That often happened when she was doing a mindless, repetitive job. Now she realized she had fixed on "Hotel California," by the Eagles. Oh great, a song about a guy who goes into a supernatural hotel. When he tries to leave, he finds out he's trapped there.

With a sigh, she kept sorting items, knowing that the song was going to stick with her until she was done.

The closet project lasted several hours. On a tear, she brought another bag upstairs and started pulling out clothes she knew she would never wear.

Next, she did forty minutes of weights and the tread-mill in her home gym.

Finally, she was hungry enough to eat something. Cooking wasn't one of her talents, but there were plenty of upscale restaurants and delis in Frederick where she could stock the fridge with gourmet carryout.

She reached for a carton of chicken salad and another of sesame noodles. While she ate, she enjoyed a playlist she'd made for herself, everything from the beautiful duet from the Pearl Fishers to James Taylor and Taylor Swift.

By the time she'd eaten, she felt better. Except that she still wasn't sure that she could get any work done tomorrow. But she did have several pieces that needed to go to a cute little shop in Saint Stephens, one of the tourist towns on Maryland's Eastern Shore. Although she often hired someone to take orders out of town, she decided to do this one by herself. Maybe a change of scenery would do her good.

After dinner, she debated sitting in front of the TV for a while. But probably she should go to bed if she was driving across the Bay Bridge in the morning. That long, high structure always made her feel like she was going to plunge through a guardrail into the bay. No, she'd better be rested and in good shape when she tackled it.

Upstairs, as she went through her nighttime ritual, she fought to dispel the notion that the man from the brick walk had somehow followed her into the house.

But she'd made him up, she told herself. He was over. Done. She was going to hang on to her sanity now.

Still, when she pulled her T-shirt over her head and unhooked her bra, she felt goose bumps pepper her arms and chest.

Glancing at the medicine cabinet, she briefly wondered if she should take an over-the-counter sleep aid, then decided that might make things worse.

She pressed the heels of her hands against her closed eyelids. Did people who were going crazy know it? Or was some evil force operating on her—offering her what she'd secretly wanted all her life?

Right. She hadn't considered *that* angle. Maybe this wasn't coming from a damaged mind. Maybe this was like what happened to people in horror movies. Only this wasn't a movie, she quickly assured herself. This was real life.

Thinking that the observation hadn't done her any good, she turned off the bedside lamp and slipped under the covers. At first, she lay rigidly in bed, waiting. When nothing happened, she relaxed fractionally. Because she was exhausted from emotional stress and all the frantic work she'd done, sleep enveloped her, and she knew nothing else until she heard the clock strike a half hour downstairs.

Which half hour? She didn't know because they all had the same one-tone bong. When she turned her head toward the window, all she saw was pitch blackness.

She stopped worrying about the time when the experience from her workshop repeated itself. In the same way the realization had crept over her before, she knew that she wasn't alone.

Oh Lord. He was here again. The last time they met, his arms had been around her. This time, although he didn't touch her, she was sure he was standing in her darkened bedroom, looking down at her. Well, why not? If he could come into the workshop, he could come into the house. Whoever or whatever he was, no locks were going to stop him.

In her workshop, he had only been an unseen presence. A feeling that he was there. On the path, she'd felt his hard contours. In the privacy of her bedroom, there was the possibility of more.

She could sense the warmth of his body. She'd thought he might be a ghost. But weren't ghosts supposed to be cold?

Too caught up in physical awareness, she was unable to puzzle that out. Everything about him teased her senses, yet this midnight visitor could not be real. In the darkened bedroom, she thought of all the imagined dangers that had plagued mankind from the dawn of time. Ghosts, demons, vampires, evil spirits. None of them seemed to fit. Would a ghost radiate warmth? Could a demon offer her the one thing in life she had always lacked and always craved? Maybe.

Did she believe in demons?

No, that was make-believe. Supernatural beings didn't come to the bedrooms of living women. But what about the delusions of that girl in the book? Her made-up demons had been as real to her as real life.

The hamster wheel of awful possibilities swirling in her head was interrupted by a voice. Well, not exactly a voice

Please, don't be afraid of me.

The words were not spoken aloud but in her mind, in a deep masculine tone.

She could be dreaming again, except that she knew she was awake.

To prove that to herself, she sat up and reached for the switch on the bedside lamp. Before she could press it, a hand jerked her fingers away, and a plea hung in the air.

"Don't." This time, she heard the word aloud.

Acknowledging him in this new way would be taking a step further into her personal psychosis, but she did it anyway.

"Why not?"

A tortured quality seeped into his words. "You will see nothing. Better to stay in the dark."

"Why are you here?"

"I need you."

The despair in his voice tore at her. Another symptom of her madness. Emotional involvement with a phantom.

And that madness was going to bring her carefully constructed life crashing down around her shoulders.

"If you're crazy, so am I."

The weary statement left her startled and shocked in a new way.

"What? Did you read my mind?"

Even as she asked the question, she knew it was true within the confines of this weird encounter.

But if she were conjuring up an imaginary companion, why not go all the way and concoct some kind of telepathic link with him? It would give her something nobody else had—to make up for all the years she'd felt so disconnected.

She had to suppress a hysterical laugh.

You're not inventing anything. Once again, the words were not spoken aloud. She dragged in a breath and let it out. This whole situation was way beyond the bounds of reality. Yet a part of her still struggled to deal with the encounter rationally.

"Who are you?" she whispered into the darkness. "Are you a ghost?

For the first time, his voice wavered as he whispered, "I don't know."

She heard his pain; more than that, she sensed it. "Why are you really here?" she demanded.

"I was drawn to you."

"From where?"

She felt him searching for the right words. "A great, cold nothingness where I was totally alone. More alone than I had ever been before." His voice hitched. "In the darkness, I saw something that pulled me forward. At first, it was only a tiny beam of light. And I knew I had to get closer. As I did, I saw it was you with your long red hair and your wonderful green eyes, and I knew I must get closer to you—or lose myself."

Her chest tightened. She had thought she was the needy one—that she had made him up to fulfill some deeply buried craving of her own. Yet he had turned the tables on her.

More proof that she had finally gone off the deep end? Or if she couldn't connect with other people, she would work out some kind of relationship with a phantom?

She had been sitting rigidly, propped against the pillows, the position adding to her tension.

Lie down. You might as well be comfortable.

Would following his directions be an acknowledgement that she thought this encounter was real?

Okay, why not go with it, if it fulfilled an unacknowledged need of her own? She wasn't hurting anybody but herself by inventing an imaginary lover for her bedroom.

A lover? Was that what she was doing because she had never had a real one who made her feel fulfilled the way women in love songs and romance novels felt?

She made a dismissive sound. Was she really that needy?

In the next moment, her muddled train of thought switched back to an earlier idea. Okay. If she had brought this phantom to her room, why not enjoy the experience while it lasted? Couldn't crazy people get some pleasure from their illness before the men in the white coats came to drag them to the funny farm?

With a sigh, she plumped up the pillows and lay back against them. He was still there, only much closer.

My lord, he was lying beside her. Surrendering to the situation, she moved over so that her shoulders and hips touched his. The contact set up a sexual pull toward him, yet at the same time, it was also strangely comforting.

Going with the fantasy or the psychotic break or whatever it was, she allowed herself to enjoy the sense of closeness. It was what she had always longed for, and he was giving it to her, even if it was only a mirage. Closing her eyes, she breathed in and out, feeling the beat of her own heart, imagining what it might be like if this visitor were real.

A shiver went through her and with it, feelings she had repressed for so long. Sexual awareness had never been a big factor in her life, and yet she felt herself responding to this invisible man as she never had before. She felt her body heating, and cursed the unwanted sensation. Why now? Why with this man who wasn't even real?

For heartbeats, she let herself build the fantasy, imagining her soulmate lying next to her—the man she had secretly wished for all her life. In the next moment, she clenched her fists.

"Stop it," she ordered herself. "This isn't real. It can't be real."

It was like building a sandcastle and watching it wash away when the tide came in.

She felt anger rising inside her, anger at herself for succumbing to this game. And anger at him. She had made him up and then pretended he was offering her something that a figment of her imagination could never give her in real life.

She knew she had been bouncing from one state of mind to the next, from fear to acceptance to sexual need, not in any particular order. None of it was entirely rational —except the fear. Now, a new determination seized her. She would not let herself sink into this madness. She would fight it.

Bent on ending the self-delusion, she let the anger

infuse her words as she said, "I am not your savior. I'm not your lover."

He didn't answer in words, but she heard him make a desperate choking sound, like a drowning man struggling to breathe underwater.

In that moment, the dream came back to her sharp and clear in all its horror. Had that been reality? Was that what had happened to *him*?

CHAPTER FOUR

Olivia's nerve endings burned as she took in the sound. It was not what she had expected. It was like a cry of anguish, a cry for help, a cry that gave her visitor a new reality that he had not possessed before. She had told herself his existence was impossible, but she knew to the depths of her soul that she had caused him pain. With that knowledge, all her resolve to drive him away crumpled.

"I'm sorry." She gripped his arm, her fingers digging into what felt like solid muscle. At the same time, she felt herself reaching out to him in a way she never had to another human being. It was like making an intimate connection that had been impossible—until he made something inside her unfurl. He had said he needed her. Unaccountably, it seemed she needed him, too.

As much to reassure herself as him, she whispered, "It's all right."

He answered with a harsh laugh. "You're just saying that. It will never be all right."

She could have asked him why, but she didn't want to hear the answer.

"We'll make it okay," she soothed, feeling an overwhelming need to take away his pain. Before she could stop herself, she rolled toward him, reaching out to clasp his body. He had warned her before not to turn on the light. This time, she was the one who would rather not take the chance of finding out that he was an illusion.

But how could he be? How could an illusion feel the pain she had heard in his cry? She couldn't answer the question, but she knew it was better not to try and see him, better to let her other senses take over.

At first, he held himself rigid in her arms, but her hands seemed to relax him. As he became more pliant, she became bolder.

Eyes closed, she hung on to him, stroking her hands up and down his arms. They were well-muscled as though he was accustomed to manual labor. Or he was like her and had a home gym. She traced broad shoulders, then reached up to run her fingers against what felt like a few days' growth of beard.

When he sighed in acquiescence, she let herself enjoy what she was doing, tracing the shape of his chin, which jutted brashly and had a cleft in the center. Traveling upward, she felt a nicely proportioned nose between high cheekbones. His eyes were closed, and she felt his thick lashes like small brushes. Above his brow, she encountered springy hair that must have some curl. What color was it, she wondered.

As he let her continue the exploration, she grew surer of herself, stroking his high cheekbones, his lips.

"Can I touch you?" he asked, his voice thick.

The question sent a little frisson through her. She didn't want to think about where this might lead, yet at the same time, she craved his touch.

"All right," she managed to say.

She felt him roll to his side, before a calloused finger explored her face the way she had done with him.

He stroked her cheeks, her nose, her closed eyelids, then found her lips, sweeping back and forth. Involuntarily, her lips parted, and he slipped a finger inside, encountering sensitive tissue that no one else had touched this way before.

Again, she felt heat building inside herself, and suddenly, in addition to the heat, came memories that must be from his past.

She gasped when she saw him as a boy, running along a dock, clambering down into a cabin cruiser, and watching as a man cast off—ignoring the arrival of the boy, who would have been left behind if he'd been late. His father, she knew because she caught his thoughts. When he grew up, he would not be like his dad. Always sad. Always on the edge of anger.

The boat sailed out of a harbor, and she thought she might recognize the view, but she couldn't be sure. Another scene took its place. He was a little older—in a classroom. A teacher was yelling at him because he'd screwed up the spelling test so badly, and every other kid in the room was looking at him. Some thought the dressing down was funny. Some felt sorry for him. His face was hot, and he wanted to slump down in his chair, but he sat up straight and "took it like a man." That was what his father often said to him. "Take it like a man."

There were more recollections, life experiences that she could have applied to herself. Other kids pairing off in high school while he remained alone. As his memories bombarded her, she gasped. "You're like me."

"What?"

"You...relationships...people." She dragged in a breath and tried to be more coherent. "You never made a meaningful connection with anyone."

"Especially not with Dad. That was my first failure."

"No."

"What would you call it?"

She sighed. If it had been his failure, it would have been the same for her. Without answering his question, she asked, "Your mom?"

Even as she questioned, she knew that his mother had died of a septic infection days after he was born. And Dad had blamed the son for the mother's death.

That knowledge had her on the verge of tears. If her childhood had been bad, maybe his had been worse.

No, bad with a different twist. Her parents had been anxious to find out what was wrong with their only child, and at the same time, determined to control her life choices. His father had all but ignored the boy.

She heard him drag in a harsh breath as he keyed into some of the painful scenes from her own childhood.

His voice turned harsh. "They thought you were crazy."

She laughed. "And now I am."

"No."

"How would you explain...this?" She flapped her arm for emphasis.

"You might be crazy if you had made me up. But you didn't. I am...myself. I didn't come from your mind."

The conversation was starting to make her head throb.

"You're invisible," she said in exasperation. Can you prove you're real?"

"How?"

"That's the question, isn't it?"

The mattress shifted. If he had been a man, she would have said that he'd gotten out of bed. Then, to her astonishment, she saw a warm glow over by her dresser. In that light, she watched her hairbrush lift from the horizontal surface.

Sitting up to see better, she watched in amazement as the strange light came toward her and along with it the brush. Some part of her acknowledged that she should be afraid. Instead, she was fascinated. Did she see a dim outline of a man glowing faintly in the midnight bedroom? She shivered, then shivered again as she felt the brush touch her head and stroke through the long red strands.

"I love your hair," he whispered. "It's lovely."

She had challenged him to prove he wasn't a figment of her imagination. She supposed she could be making this up, too.

All her life, she had wished for someone who could bridge the gap between her and the rest of humanity. Had that wish come true—in a way that should be impossible? Was it insane to think the two of them could forge some kind of meaningful relationship? She marveled that she had even asked the question.

After suppressing a hysterical laugh, she managed to say.

"Whatever this is—it's happening too fast."

"You want me to...give you some space?"

"You'd better."

The hairbrush dropped to the floor with a clank, and she was alone in the room, feeling abandoned and confused. The way she had often felt. Only this was worse because she was the one who had rejected the overture.

CHAPTER FIVE

Olivia climbed out of bed. When she took a step, her foot tramped down on the bristles of the hairbrush, and she winced. Bending, she retrieved it with a shaky hand before returning it to the dresser. How had it gotten from where it belonged to the floor beside her bed if he hadn't carried it? She knew she hadn't gotten out of bed and brought it over. She knew she hadn't been brushing her own hair. Or had she done those things without acknowledging them?

As confusion swirled in her head, she swung her gaze around the room. Although it was too dark to see colors, she knew what they were. She had decorated this private space in soothing blues and greens to make it into a sanctuary, a place where she could shut out all the people she didn't understand and didn't want to deal with. Now it felt strangely empty. Would the man come back if she called him? Was he lurking somewhere nearby? Or perhaps he was still in the room, invisible but waiting to see what she would do now.

She climbed back into the bed, pulled up the covers, and slid down so that her face was partially obscured. After a few moments, she decided that if she thought she was going back to sleep any time soon, she was kidding herself. She was too off balance for that. She had sent the man away because it had seemed like the only sane course of action. And he had gone, leaving her with a feeling of emptiness.

The man? She had told herself he was some kind of ghost or spirit. But he had taken on a different reality. Not because she'd vaguely seen him when he'd done that trick with the lights. It was their conversation. As they'd talked, he'd taken on a personality that had only been a hint at the beginning. He had a history, feelings, and needs—just as she did. And he'd told her she could fulfill those needs.

Could he do the same for her? Too restless to lie in bed, she got up and walked to the window, where she stood staring out into the night. Glancing at her watch, she saw that it was four thirty in the morning. Really, she should try to get some sleep. But she knew it was too late for that. If she took some medication now, there was no telling when she was going to get up.

As she stared through the window with unfocused eyes, she couldn't help thinking that she had made a mistake. Her visitor had offered her the thing she had always craved. And she had been too afraid to accept the offer.

After dithering for several minutes, she whispered into the darkness.

"If you can hear me, come back."

At first, nothing happened and she felt disappointment settle over her like a heavy cloak. Then she sensed a presence behind her.

"Where were you?"

In the darkness. Waiting and hoping that you'd change your mind.

She wanted to be angry that he had been confident enough to linger nearby. Instead, she was secretly glad.

No, it wasn't secret. She couldn't keep a secret when her thoughts were open to him.

That was a strange concept for a woman who had never felt a deep connection to anyone. And here she was, totally open and vulnerable.

She caught the warmth of his body behind her and told herself he couldn't be a ghost if he was warm. Reaching back, she touched his chest, her hand encountering what felt like a T-shirt. Sliding farther down, she found rougher fabric. Jeans, she thought. She'd wondered if he would be naked. It seemed that he was dressed in ordinary clothing.

"How do I know you're not going to get me to...to want you to stay here and then disappear?" she heard herself ask.

He sighed. "I guess you can't. But the more we..." he stopped and searched for a word, "*interact*, the more I'm anchored to you."

"What does that mean?" she shot back.

Several seconds passed before he answered. "When I first woke up, there was nothingness all around me—except that I sensed you and moved toward you. Then I found you, and I wasn't in the darkness any longer. I was back on earth.

"You weren't on...earth when you were in the darkness?"

"I don't think so."

When he began speaking again, she sensed that he hated that admission. "Things began to change. First, I just watched you."

"I knew you were there."

"Then I caught you when you fell. I was surprised that I could do it." He seemed to drag in a breath and let it out. "Each thing we did, each thing we said, made me feel more real. I mean, when I was in the darkness, I could hardly sense myself. Now, if I hold up my hand, I can see it. Or I can look down and see my feet. I feel them, too. And I can touch you and feel you." There was satisfaction and wonder in his voice.

The admission sent goose bumps peppering her skin.

She thought back to when she'd first been aware of him. He'd been a vague presence. Something hovering around her that she couldn't quite identify. Then they'd spoken...touched...and he'd become more solid. How far could she go with that? There had to be a limit. No matter how much she craved it, it was a leap too far to believe that she could make him real by the force of her will.

"Is it?" he asked.

She cursed herself for the kind of blind hope that blossomed inside her. But okay, maybe she couldn't do it alone. What about together? How far could the two of them take this?

She knew he caught the thought. Knew he sensed her fear that she would be embracing the madness she had always feared?

Not madness. An opportunity—that no one else has. As he spoke, he pressed the front of his body against the back of hers, teaching her every hard line of his form.

She felt heat coming off of him—transferring itself to her.

When he stepped away, she had to stifle a cry. Swiftly, she turned to face him. It was still dark in the room, but now she could see him more clearly than she had before. He was wearing the jeans and T-shirt she had touched earlier, like a man who had dressed for outdoor work or perhaps simply a leisurely morning around the house. Well, what did she expect, choir robes?

An opportunity, he repeated.

"Like what?"

He held up his hand, moving it closer to her, and she saw little sparks flickering around his fingers. She raised her own hand and felt the sparks leap from his fingers to hers.

"Oh!"

The sensation tingled along her nerve endings, not just her fingers but spreading through her body.

"Don't."

Are you afraid?

I should be.

You like it.

She wanted to lie, but she knew there was no point in forming those words—not when her thoughts were so open to him.

Why not take the next step?

She had always felt less than normal. Now her phantom was offering her the opportunity to be more. Somewhere in her mind, she knew she should be afraid. She pushed away the fear and embraced what he was offering. Even if this whole illusion ended when the sun came up, she'd regret it for the rest of her life if she walked away now.

That might be a rationalization. Yet she knew she had made a decision.

Sensing her agreement, he closed the distance between them. When he opened his arms, she came into them, feeling his well-muscled body again. But that wasn't all. Now she felt the erection straining at the front of his jeans, telling her what he wanted. She closed her eyes and lowered her head to his shoulder, clinging to him, deliberately shutting out her sense of sight again.

With her eyes closed, the reality of him overwhelmed her. The sensation of her lover holding her in his arms was perfect, and when his hands stroked up and down her back and reached to caress the curve of her bottom, she felt heat flare in every cell of her body.

A small voice in her mind told her she was crazy to be

doing this. But the voice was wiped out by the sensations coursing through her. Unable to hold still, she moved against him, striving for more intimate contact.

When he turned her in his arms, she cried out in protest until he made his intentions clear. His hands came up to clasp her breasts, cupping and shaping them before he found her nipples and drew his thumbs across them.

She felt wet heat between her legs, more heat than she had ever felt in her life. Her breathing accelerated, and she found she needed to drag in air to keep herself grounded. It didn't help that somewhere inside her head, a pain throbbed in time to the frantic beating of her heart.

She might have pulled away, but he held her fast. She was still dressed in the T-shirt and yoga pants she had worn to bed, but they were no impediment to his maddening fingers. He reached right through her clothing, and she felt his touch on her naked flesh.

When his fingers brushed against the tight points of her breasts, she wanted more. He obliged, taking her nipples between his fingers and thumbs, pressing and twisting, increasing the need for even more.

"That's right, let yourself feel everything I can give you."

Hearing the husky words was a spur to her arousal. She wanted that. She wanted everything he was offering.

"Lord, you are so sexy."

"It was never like this before." Her own words came out as a gasp. *Not with anyone.*

Again, the thought skittered through her mind that she

was so alone that she had driven herself crazy. But his voice in her head soothed her.

I want this as much as you do. For myself. Not because you invented me.

Want what? Exactly.

We should find out. The silent voice hitched. *Or should I stop?*

She should end the madness before it went any further. But she was way beyond making rational decisions.

When he heard the decision in her mind, he clasped her shoulders.

Take off your clothes.

Why? You can touch me through them.

I want you naked.

I'm standing in front of the window.

There's no one out there to see.

Without giving herself time to think, she did as he asked. She felt his warmth behind her, and in front, the coolness coming from the window glass. It made her nipples pucker more than they had been before.

Again, his knowing fingers did the things she craved, wringing a cry from her.

She had gone this far with some of the men she had dated. She had even had one disastrous night in bed with a guy she met at a bar, after she'd drunk enough to stop thinking about what she was doing. It had never felt good enough to want to continue. But he was bringing forth feelings in her that she had never experienced before.

It wasn't simply sexual need building inside her body. Her mind was tuned to his more solidly now.

He knew exactly what she needed, and he was giving her what she craved. As she arched against him and her arousal built, she drew knowledge from his mind. Knowledge that had been hidden from him.

There was a moment of startling understanding for both of them.

She was the one who spoke, feeling excitement sweep over her. "Your name is Travis. Travis Carson. You have a boat named *The Far Horizon*." And she knew that he had picked the name because of a longing that he had known he could never fulfill. Until now.

The reality of that insight seemed to explode inside her, and with the throbbing came a headache that was almost unbearable.

She felt him start to pull away in fear—fear for her. *God, what am I doing to you? I have to stop.*

But her instinct was stronger than his fear. *No! If you do, you'll make it worse.*

A kind of desperation seized her as she grabbed one of his hands and pulled it to her center—the part of her that most needed his attention.

You're sure.

Don't stop.

Responding to her urgency, he pressed his fingers to the throbbing place between her legs, then slid downward through her wet folds. She felt two fingers slip deep inside her, stroking in and out in a maddening rhythm.

A small part of her mind wondered how he could do that as he stood in back of her. But most of her didn't care how he was doing it. Frantically, she moved her hips against his hand, striving to find satisfaction.

"I know. I know," he answered, as he pressed and stroked, his every move guided by her unspoken needs. She caught his exaltation as he brought her higher and higher, and she sensed that he was experiencing what she felt in his own body.

He kept up the maddening attentions, one hand at her center, the other playing with her breasts until she felt an explosion of sensation shake her, rocking her being.

She collapsed back against him. If he had not been holding her, she would not have been able to stand. She leaned against him, her breath coming in gasps.

Across the room, she heard a sharp crack. Her eyes flew open, and she saw shards of glass from the bulb in the bedside lamp. As the noise faded, the sparks she had seen before swam around the room in an excited dance.

"My God, what?"

"Something spectacular."

It had been that, all right. She had experienced an orgasm the likes of which she had never imagined, and with that came a stab of guilt.

"You..."

"I felt it through you," he answered. "Like nothing I've ever felt in my life. All through my body, not just a spasm in my cock."

The sparks around them had faded. He held her up as

she wobbled toward the bed and fell onto the horizontal surface, where she lay with her eyes closed, breathing hard.

He came down beside her, gathering her to him.

"Thank you," he breathed.

"I think I'm the one who should do the thanking."

"Not worth arguing about."

She lay in his arms, still trying to take in what had happened. She felt different now. The headache had vanished like a storm cloud after a torrential shower, and she knew that something momentous had happened to her.

FAR AWAY IN NEW ORLEANS, Rachel Gregory wavered on suddenly unsteady legs and dropped the tarot card she was holding.

Her husband, Jake, was instantly at her side. "Rachel, what is it? Are you sick? What?"

When she didn't answer, he swept her up in his arms and lowered himself into a comfortable chair where he cradled her in his lap.

She had come to her shop because she had sensed something strange happening, and she needed her cards to help her figure out what it was. Jake had come along because she was acting strangely, and he hadn't wanted to leave her alone.

She nestled against him, dragging in drafts of air. Ever since they'd met outside the murder scene of a clandestine operative, they'd forged a bond that neither one of them had ever expected to experience.

Both of them had been alone—just like all of the children born from the crazy experiments of Dr. Douglas Solomon. His fertility clinic had been a way to obtain human embryos he could use to create super-intelligent children. The experiment had failed. And when the government cut off his grant money, nobody realized that his brain experiments had created something else: telepaths who felt utterly unable to form a meaningful relationship with anyone until they met another of Dr. Solomon's children. Then everything changed—for the spectacularly better or spectacularly worse. Either they forged an unbreakable bond, or they died together in bed from a cerebral hemorrhage.

Rachel and Jake, along with a small group of other telepaths, were the lucky ones. At least lucky that they had survived and bonded. The downside was that they'd found themselves pursued by evil forces bent on controlling them or wiping them out.

The couple spent about half their time at the colony of telepaths they'd established at the plantation Gabriella Bordeaux had inherited from her mother. The rest of each week, they were in New Orleans, where Jake attended to his restaurant and antique business, while Rachel did tarot card reading in her shop in the French Quarter.

Rachel blinked up at her husband. "I'm all right," she murmured.

"What happened? Did...did you sense another couple making it past the initial crisis?"

Rachel had extraordinary mental powers and seemed to sense when two more of Dr. Solomon's children had forged a link to each other. This time, she looked perplexed.

"What?" Jake pressed.

"It's not like with the others."

He grimaced. "Are...are you saying that one of them made it through their first lovemaking—and the other didn't?"

"No, that's not it." Rachel licked her dry lips. "It wasn't the same as with us or any of the others. I think...I think..."

When she hesitated, he urged, "Just spit it out."

"Okay, I know it sounds impossible, but I'm pretty sure one of them was already dead."

His curse filled the small room, "You must be mistaken. How could...a living person bond with a deceased one?"

"I'm just telling you what I sensed, although I could be dead wrong."

"Dead wrong. Yeah." His laugh wasn't quite steady. After several moments of hesitation, he asked, "Um, which one...um...do you think is a ghost?"

She could tell from his shaky voice that he wasn't entirely committed to the concept.

"I'm not sure. They're pretty far away."

CHAPTER SIX

Olivia stayed pressed to Travis, her eyes closed, unable to face him and yet unable to move away. He must have sensed that, too. Without speaking, he helped her get under the covers and stayed beside her.

Her face heated when she thought of what she had let him do—what she had begged him to do. She had given herself completely to him in a way she had never even been able to imagine before.

She had read in books and seen TV shows where the characters had an awkward "morning after." This must be the one that took the prize. Even though it was still dark, it *was* technically morning.

She knew he caught her thought when he answered, "I wanted that as much as you did. And like you, I didn't understand how much I was asking for."

"But I was the only one who..." She let the rest of the sentence trail off.

"Giving you so much pleasure was...mind-blowing."

"But..."

"When you came, I felt what you did. It was as good for me as it was for you." He reached for her hand and knitted his fingers with hers.

She heard a teasing smile in his voice. "Now I know what an orgasm is like for a woman. You feel it all over your body...not just *there.*"

Even after the earthquake of a climax he had given her, or maybe because of it, the conversation was becoming much too intimate. He must have picked that up from her mind because he changed the subject. "It wasn't just great sex. You gave me a gift. I know who I am now."

She heard the wonder in his voice. "Being with you has changed me."

"Changed both of us." She felt her excitement growing. "Remember, I now know you have a boat, *The Far Horizon.* I even know where it is. I can go there and find..."

He didn't let her finish the sentence.

"No."

"Why not? Do you have something there that you don't want me to see?"

"Of course not. But getting anywhere near my boat could be dangerous. Stay away from it."

She was wondering how he could keep her from going there, and she knew he caught that thought as well.

"I can't stop you. I'm pleading with you to stay away. I don't want anything to happen to you."

His obvious panic tugged at her. *Like the same thing that happened to you?*

The questions hung in the air. In the darkness, she turned to him. She knew she could go prowling through his thoughts, but she didn't want to do it.

Calmer than she had been in days, she kept her silence and snuggled against him. She had gone through some kind of strange adjustment. When she'd first sensed him hovering around her, she'd been afraid of him. Tonight he had taken an important place in her life, and she accepted that new reality.

She would have sworn she heard him drag in a breath and let it out. Could he really do that?

"Well, I'm not exactly breathing, but I can...make it seem like I am."

"Okay."

She knew they were both avoiding a painful revelation.

Finally he said, "I remember more than my name. I know what happened to me."

"Tell me."

"It's...brutal," he warned.

"I need to know if we're going to make whoever did this...pay."

"Maybe we can't."

"We're not just going to accept it."

This time he was the one who answered, "Okay."

She felt her heart start to pound as she waited.

"It started off like an ordinary overnight charter. Three men arranged for a fishing trip. I took them out past the bay to the ocean. When we were out there, they jumped me."

"Who were they?"

The guy who seemed to be in charge said he was Andrew. Another was Pete. The third was Lambert."

"What were their last names?"

"It probably doesn't matter. I can't believe they would turn out to be their real names. Maybe the first names they were using were even false."

She wanted to ask more questions, but instead, a vivid picture leaped into her mind. She saw the trio coming down the dock, dressed in jeans and polo shirts, each carrying a gym bag, as though they were ready for an overnight fishing trip out on the ocean. Andrew and Pete were normal-sized men. Lambert looked like he could have been a linebacker for the NFL. They seemed to be in high spirits, but he had thought there was something "off" about them. Only when it was too late did he realize that the vibe came from nerves. They were tasked with pulling off a big charade, and they were worried about somehow screwing it up. It would have been easier if they could have just killed the target. But they'd been ordered to bring him in alive.

From Travis's memory, she saw the scene play out in her mind. They'd all been trailing their fishing lines in the water. When Travis had started for the companionway to bring up some beers, they'd all dropped the fishing pretense. Lambert had snuck up behind him and grabbed his arms. Pete and Andrew approached from the front. Even taken by surprise, Travis put up a pretty good fight.

His first response was to shake off Lambert, who had clamped on to his arms. Travis was strong, and he bent from the waist, ducking down so that he could raise the guy in the air and throw him over his head, slamming him onto the deck. He landed with a nasty thump, howling in pain. But the other two men moved in to intercept their target.

Even while he was fighting off the assault, Travis was still battling confusion. These guys had chartered his boat for a routine fishing trip, and now they were attacking him for no discernible reason. He didn't know any of them. Had somebody with a beef against him sent them?

"What the hell's going on?" he shouted.

The trio ignored his question as they went on the defensive.

"Watch out," one of them warned. "He's stronger than he looks."

"Too bad we can't just shoot him."

"The boss wants him alive—with no sign of foul play."

As they closed in, he grabbed Pete and managed to toss him over the side. Now it was only two against one.

Taking a fighting stance, he readied himself for another assault. Unfortunately, it came from behind.

From where he lay on the deck, Andrew kicked out a foot, tangling with one of Travis's legs and yanking backwards. By that time, Pete had climbed back into the boat and joined the attack again. As Travis fought to keep his balance, the other two closed in. A sap materialized in Pete's hand. He brought it down on Travis's head, and that was the last he knew until he came to, tied up in the back of what looked like a delivery van.

His head hurt like a son of a bitch, but he started trying to loosen the bonds that held him. He had the advantage of having worked with knots all his life, and he had made good progress on his hands when the van came to an abrupt stop. Unfortunately, there simply wasn't enough time for him to effect an escape.

When Pete and Andrew hauled him out and saw that he was well on the way to freeing his hands, the big man gave him a slap across the face that knocked him silly. Once again, he blacked out.

He looked at Olivia, and she could sense the question forming in his mind. "It gets worse from here. Are you sure you want me to go on?"

Worse? That had been pretty bad, but she answered "Yes," struggling to hold the word steady. To reassure herself, she burrowed closer to him and closed her eyes. His arms came up to clasp her, and he felt as solid as if...

She didn't let herself finish the thought.

He continued the way he had begun, letting her see what had happened to him next.

He'd awakened, still dressed in his boat clothes. He was strapped tightly into a sturdy chair with a padded back and seat and tubular arms and legs. When he tested his bonds, he discovered that there was no hope of getting free.

A man who had been sitting in an easy chair got up and strode over to him. "You're awake."

Travis blinked and sat up straighter, trying to bring the

situation into sharper focus. It seemed the men who had chartered the boat had been planning to bring him here all along.

He took in his surroundings. Except for the easy chair, the rest of the room was pretty sterile. There were several cabinets along one wall, containing medicine bottles. This could have been in a doctor's exam room—with a standard table over to one side. He didn't much like the setup.

"Who are you? Why the hell am I here?" he asked, struggling to keep any quiver out of his voice. His heart was starting to pound, and he was pretty sure he was in deep trouble. Wracking his brain, he tried to figure out why. He'd never seen this man before. Didn't know him. But the guy must have some reason for having him brought here. Was it something specific about him? Or would any victim have done? The latter seemed unlikely since the guy had gone to a lot of trouble to capture him.

Instead of answering, the inquisitor said, "Sorry my men roughed you up."

"Who are you? What do you want?"

"You can call me Smith, if you need a name."

"But it's not your real name," Travis shot back.

His captor shrugged, and Travis didn't like the feel of the casual gesture. He studied the man. He appeared to be in his sixties or possibly older, with salt-and-pepper hair, a lined face, and a malevolent gleam in his pale eyes. He knew he was totally in charge of this situation.

Travis might have screamed for help, but he was sure that wasn't going to do him any good. Was there any reasoning with this guy? Had he been captured by a lunatic? Or was there some rational thinking behind this elaborate scheme?

"Why am I here?" he tried again.

"To provide me with the information I've been seeking."

"And then what?"

"Then we'll see."

Travis didn't like the sound of that, either, but he was completely at this guy's mercy.

"Your mother went down to Louisiana for fertility treatments," Smith suddenly said.

"How do you know?"

"I have the records from the Solomon Clinic. That's where she went."

Olivia intruded into the scene with a gasp. "Fertility clinic," she choked out.

Travis looked at her. "What?"

"I was born as a result of fertility treatments. Do you think? I mean..." Her voice trailed off before she said, "I'd better shut up and listen."

"We could stop," Travis offered, and she knew that was what he wanted to do.

She shook her head. "I have to know."

He made a rough sound before bringing her back into the scene with Smith. His captor was saying, "You aren't on the list of children whose mothers kept the agreement they signed before the treatments. They were supposed to bring the children back for testing, but yours never did."

"Because she died when I was born. And I'm sure as hell my dad wasn't gonna honor any agreement she signed."

"So we've cleared that up."

"Did you know that's how you were born?"

Travis wondered why he should answer this guy's questions. He could think of several good reasons—the first being that he was tied to a chair, and he was probably going to get the crap beaten out of him if he didn't cooperate."

"And you don't know that Dr. Solomon was doing brain experiments on the unborn children."

If Travis could have jumped up in surprise, he would have. "No."

"I believe his goal was to create super smart individuals, but that experiment turned out to be a dud. When the children were tested, they had the standard IQ spread."

Travis shook his head, trying to work his way through the strange revelations that were hitting him like bowling balls.

"But the doctor's experiments did have an unexpected effect. They created children with special powers. Do you have any?"

"What? No."

"You can't move objects with your mind?"

"Huh?"

"Or call up any lightning bolts to zap people?"

"Are you crazy?"

Ignoring the question, Smith went on. "You never read

anybody's thoughts? Or made anybody bend to your will? Or slowed down time?"

Travis tried to wrap his mind around the crazy questions. "None of that's possible."

The man continued with rapid-fire questions. "Do you have intuitions? Do you make special connections with people? Can you talk to them without speaking? Do you think of things that are going to happen and find out they come true?'

"Jesus," Travis exclaimed. "Nothing like that."

Smith was still talking—babbling on with more outlandish suggestions. Then he switched gears and confided, "You know, all the children turned out to be loners. Mostly kept to themselves until they met one of the other subjects. Then—boom. And away they go. That's made it really hard to catch any of them. Safer this way."

The words hardly registered. Travis was thinking about special powers and coming up blank. But it seemed that Smith was talking to himself now.

"I'm not sure every one of the couples has all of those skills. I think some of them can do some things, and some others. But let's try to find what you've got."

While Travis was wondering what was coming next, Smith was saying, "From what I've observed, I believe there is a sexual component. I mean, the abilities might be triggered by sexual contact. I don't have another subject here, but maybe I can use hypnosis to create the right circumstance for you to manifest."

Olivia watched the scene unfold with growing horror.

"You still want to watch?" Travis asked, and she could tell from the uneven note in his voice that he was hoping she'd call an end to the revelation.

He shuddered. "It gets kind of nasty from here on out."

GABE BOWMAN PULLED to a stop in front of a red brick two-story in Berlin, Maryland, and checked the house number. Yes, this was the right place. Decorah Security had sent him to the Eastern Shore to check out a missing person's report that had been ignored by the police.

It was a routine assignment. Nothing paranormal. The werewolves who worked for the agency were most likely to get those, although Gabe had been on some pretty unusual cases—stuff that the general public would consign to the realm of fantasy or science fiction. But from his work with the Decorah, Gabe knew that you could never discount the weird. As far as he was concerned, that was one of the perks of working for Frank Decorah, like the time Gabe had been in on the takedown of a clandestine military base where the commanding officer was into some highly illegal stuff. Specifically, the growing of clones to send off on suicide missions. I mean, why sacrifice a real human being when you could make an expendable copy?

They had rescued one of the poor bastards. He'd been a mess when they recovered him, but he'd joined the agency and turned out to be one of their prime operatives.

Gabe knew Frank Decorah was very particular about which of his people he sent where. This seemed like a routine assignment, but maybe there was something special about it that Gabe would figure out along the way. He hoped so. He wasn't keen on trying to track down a guy who had probably figured he had good reason to take off and cut his losses. On the other hand, perhaps Travis Carson had met with foul play. But no use jumping to conclusions until he had some solid facts.

He studied the house. It looked old, probably dating back to the early 20th century, but it was well-maintained. The wide wood trim had a new coat of paint, and the grounds were neatly manicured with flower beds running in straight lines along the front of the porch and along the brick walk in what he thought of as the German style, orderly and standing to attention.

After ringing the bell, he waited for several minutes before he heard footsteps shuffling toward the door. First, he saw a gnarled hand pull aside the curtain at the sidelight so a shadowy figure could peer out. Apparently he passed inspection, because the door was opened cautiously by a woman who looked to be in her late sixties or early seventies with a lined face and white hair pinned neatly up in a bun.

"Yes?"

"I'm Gabe Bowman from Decorah Security. Are you Lydia Wilder?"

"Yes." She gave him a dubious inspection, taking in his

dark hair, dark eyes, and face he had contrived to age a bit with a neatly trimmed beard.

"Aren't you too young to be a detective?"

"I'm a graduate of the University of Maryland law enforcement program and worked for the Montgomery County police for four years before joining Decorah Security."

"Why aren't you still with the police? Did you get fired or something?"

Thinking this was a bad way to start an interview, he sighed. "I was in a department where a lot of guys were in front of me for promotion. Then Frank Decorah, the head of the agency, offered me a job and I took it."

"All right. You might as well come in." The woman stepped aside so he could enter.

After locking the door behind them, she led him through an entry hall with a dining room on one side and a sitting room on the other. The sofa and chairs sported cream-colored doilies on the arms. When she lowered herself into a straight-back rocker, he took a wing-back opposite.

"Ms. Wilder..."

"That's Miss Wilder. I never met a man I thought was worth giving up my independence for. I made a good living for myself as an executive assistant at White and Pendelton," she said, naming a well-known manufacturer of power tools that had its home office on the Eastern Shore.

He might have apologized for the mistake if he hadn't been afraid she'd take it the wrong way.

Instead, he simply said, "I'm going to take some notes."

"Go ahead."

"You say your nephew disappeared about two weeks ago?" he began.

"Yes."

"How did you realize he was missing?"

"Usually, he calls me every other week. We don't have a set day because he takes people out on fishing expeditions. When he didn't call, I got concerned. I left messages, then drove over to St. Stephens where he keeps his boat. It's in its usual slip. He's not there."

"What about his home?"

"He's got a small house that he inherited from his father. He wasn't there either."

"His car?"

"It's a Toyota Camry. I didn't see it in either place."

"So he could have driven away somewhere."

"That's what the police think. They say they put out an all-points bulletin."

"But nobody's seen the car."

"Correct."

"You don't think he could have just taken off for somewhere?"

"No. He would have told me." She sighed. "That boy had a tough life. His mother died when he was born, and his father always blamed him. I guess I was the only person who cared about him, and his father never let me get really close."

Gabe nodded. "Does he have a girlfriend? Did you try to contact his friends?"

"Travis has always been a loner. It's his father's fault as much as anyone's. I told Marian not to marry that man, but she wouldn't listen to me. She was all excited about Rob Carson." Travis's aunt stopped and sighed. "He did have some good qualities. When she had trouble getting pregnant, he let her go to some big-deal fertility clinic in Louisiana, of all places. Of course, it all went to hell when she died. Rob was bitter, you know."

"I can imagine." Gabe had his own family issues, like his parents, who thought law enforcement wasn't prestigious enough for their son. And a private detective was another notch down. They didn't subscribe to the concept that work you loved was worth more than your job title.

"Where's the father now?"

"Drank himself into an early grave—good riddance. The astonishing thing is that he had a fair amount of cash stashed away. Travis was able to trade up for a bigger boat than the one Rob left him."

Gabe nodded, taking it in. "Could someone have killed Travis for his money and hidden the body?"

"That's what I think. That boy kept his private business close to his chest, but someone could have known that he was a lot better off than met the eye."

Gabe wondered if the money was still in his bank account. The aunt wouldn't have been able to get that kind of information, but he could.

"Anything else you think is important to know about

him?" he asked. "Was he in any kind of trouble, that you know of?"

"No, He was strictly on the up-and-up."

Gabe figured that might be true, or it might not. Carson could be using his boat for smuggling, for all the aunt knew.

"Did he go off on long trips?"

"No. He stayed close to home base."

Gabe asked more questions and got directions to the house as well as specific directions for locating the boat. Both were in St. Stephens.

In the early years, its economy had relied on crabbing and clamming. Now the residents made most of their money from tourists who crossed the Bay Bridge to take in the small town's seaside atmosphere.

"I'm counting on you to find out what happened to him."

Gabe might have said, "Let's hope it's not bad news."

As he left Miss Wilder, he was thinking about which he should try first—the boat or the house.

CHAPTER SEVEN

Olivia's throat was so clogged that she could barely speak, but she managed to say, "I want to know the rest of it."

She knew Travis had been hoping she would tell him to forget about the rest, but she had to *know*.

"All right."

She watched as the chair Travis was strapped into slowly changed its shape so that he was lying down, still firmly restrained.

Smith went to one of the cabinets, got out a hypodermic needle and a small bottle of liquid. After filling the syringe, he found a vein in Travis's arm and injected the stuff. Pretty quickly, he began to feel woozy and at the same time aroused.

Smith gave him a knowing smile. "Excellent. Are you attracted to men or women?"

Travis turned his head away.

"From studying your recent activities, I assume it's

women. I mean, I know you haven't hooked up with any guys you've met at a bar. But you've had liaisons with women."

"What? Have you been spying on me?" Travis managed to say.

"Of course. I wouldn't have gone ahead with this operation unless I was completely sure of a successful outcome. Now I'm going to put you into a trance. The medication I've given you makes you susceptible to that." His voice became rhythmic. "In a moment, I'm going to leave the room. Someone else will come in—a beautiful woman. She will walk to your side and stand over you." He continued the sing-song, persuasive cadence. "She's also one of the children from the Solomon Clinic. She's here to fulfill your sexual desires. Sex with her will be better than anything you've ever experienced. You're going to enjoy your time with her—very much."

Travis shook his head, turning his gaze away again, trying to fight the man's lulling voice and the temptations he was offering. But he now felt like he was swimming through thick syrup, struggling to breathe. He heard the door open and close, and he was thankful to be alone. But he was still a captive, drifting on the man's words and the drug.

He closed his eyes, sinking toward sleep. Until a new voice called his name. A woman.

"Travis. Travis, I've been so anxious to get together with you."

He snapped awake. "Huh?" he asked in a groggy voice, trying to bring her image into focus.

"We're going to have a wonderful time," she said in a sultry whisper. Smith had been the only one in the room with him. Now he had vanished, and as he had promised, a gorgeous, desirable woman was standing exactly where his captor had been.

She seemed very real, but where had she come from? Who was she? His vision wavered as he tried to study her. She couldn't be real, he told himself, but here she was, big as life and twice as tempting. Her hair was long and blonde. Her eyes were startlingly blue. Her lips were pouty. As she leaned over him, her full breasts swayed toward him, almost spilling out from the low neckline of her lacy white blouse. If he could have lifted his hands, he would have reached for them.

No, this wasn't...

He blinked again, trying to clear his vision.

"I'm going to bring you to the peak of pleasure. Do you understand?" she promised, her voice curling around him.

Again, he questioned his vision. But as her voice and her touch enveloped him, he was helpless to resist the suggestions she was sending him. It didn't matter who or what she was—only that she was here instead of Smith. He had fought against Smith as best he could. There was no way to fight her.

"My name is Cynthia," she cooed.

He had never gotten into what he would consider a meaningful relationship with a woman, but he had the normal male urges. And this woman was a tempting sexual partner. He licked his suddenly dry lips as he felt his heart rate quicken.

"You and I are going to bond." As she spoke, she opened the button at the top of his jeans and opened the zipper before pushing down his briefs so that she could pull out his cock. He was already hard.

"Nice," she approved.

He didn't want this. He wanted to get away from her. But restrained on the table, he could do nothing to escape from this crude advance.

As Cynthia began to stroke him, she spoke in a lilting voice. "I'm another one of the children from the Solomon Clinic. I can read your mind. I know what you want." She laughed softly. "Well, that's obvious, isn't it. You want to fuck me. But I can't release your arms, so we'll just have to do it this way."

"No."

"You don't really want to resist me, do you? Relax, let me give you the ultimate pleasure."

He wanted to defy her, but the drugs coursing through his system had taken over his mind. There was no way he could battle the woman or the sexual stimulation. Her voice droned on, telling him that they were bonding, that now they would be able to do all the things Smith had told him about.

His whole body trembled as he felt himself pulled into the sexual scenario. He was enflamed. Frantic with need. Trembling on the edge of release, but Cynthia teased him, bringing him close to climax, then stopping her maddening ministrations before he could come.

He groaned. "Please."

"Please what?"

"You're driving me insane."

"Is that good or bad?" she murmured.

When he didn't answer, she went on. "Do you feel it? Are we bonding? Will it happen when you come?"

The drugs made it impossible to ignore her voice or her maddening hand as it teased his cock. Finally, when he thought he couldn't take another moment of her knowing touch, she sped up her strokes, urging him toward climax. He cried out in relief as he came in a burst of guilty pleasure, then lay drained and panting on the chair-table.

Cynthia's face hung over him, her breasts within easy reach if he could have moved his arms. "I guess you didn't get the headache," she said in a dry voice.

"Wha...what?"

"I threw some couples together." She stopped and laughed. "Like one of the kids from the clinic was a twin, and his brother was collateral damage in a drug hit. He'd been trying for years to find out who was responsible. I sent him information that pointed him in the right direction. To a New Orleans high society type who was also a drug smuggler. His fiancée happened to be another one of Solomon's spawn." She sobered. "I almost captured them, but it went bad in the end. And then there were the ones who didn't survive their first mutual sexual experience. They were the ones who died in bed together. Maybe having sex was too much for them, or maybe they chickened out, and that's what did it. The cause of death was cerebral hemorrhages, according to the autopsies."

The words were going over Travis's head. He had no idea what she was talking about.

But she pressed on—probing for information he couldn't give her. "Did coming with your mate change anything for you? Can we merge our minds? Try to untie the bonds on your wrists. You want to get free, don't you?"

"Yes." The syllable came out like a low growl.

"Then untie the knots. Or maybe you can burn the rope." Her insistent voice stopped for a moment. "Well, that might not be prudent. You don't want to burn yourself."

With every shred of determination he possessed, Travis tried to loosen the knots. He had to get away from this woman—from this nightmare situation. But even after exerting a tremendous effort, he simply had no power to break free.

"What about a thunderbolt?" she asked. "Use your mind to throw one across the room. Or throw one at me. You want to do that, don't you?"

"Yes," he managed between clenched teeth. She had taken advantage of him. Aroused him. Raped him. And he wanted to make her pay for what she had done.

Desperation made him redouble his efforts, but he might as well have been trying to throw a cannonball. Nothing happened. It couldn't happen. There was nothing different about him. He was the same man who had awakened as a captive in this room

"Maybe if we try a jolt of chemical stimulant," a voice muttered. It was Smith again. The sexy Cynthia had vanished. Had she really been there? He didn't know.

Travis felt another needle jabbing into a vein, and his whole body seized. "Do it," Smith shouted. "Do something. Don't just lie there like a sorry victim. Free yourself. Don't you have the power to do it?"

He *wanted to.* With every ounce of will in his body, he *wanted to.*

Desperately, Travis tried to find a way to accomplish the impossible, feeling all his muscles strain as he strove to pull himself free. But there was no amount of effort that could make any difference. Finally exhausted, he fell back against the table.

He heard Smith sigh. "Well, we gave it the old college try. I guess a simulation isn't going to work. Too bad. I'm afraid I'm going to have to examine some of your brain tissue to see if I find anything unusual."

As Travis heard the sound of a power drill firing to life, a jolt of fear shot through him.

"Does that inspire you to try harder?" Smith asked.

It did. If there had been any way to manipulate his physical surroundings, he would have done it. But he simply couldn't manage it. All he could do was lie there as the whirring of the drill came closer.

He screamed, then screamed again as he felt the metal bit jab into his skull.

CHAPTER EIGHT

This time, it was Olivia who screamed. She sat up with a jerk and started to push herself off the bed, afraid that she was going to throw up on the covers. Somehow, she brought the nausea under control.

Eyes closed, she collapsed back against the pillows as sobs began to wrack her. Terrifying and disgusting moments from the scene with Smith played over and over in her mind. That man must not possess any shred of morality—or he never could have done those horrible things to another human being.

Travis reached for her and wrapped her in his embrace. "I'm sorry," he whispered. "I'm so sorry. I'm sorry you had to see that." He made an angry sound. "To see my shame."

Her hands tightened on him, and somehow she managed to get words out between sobs. "Oh Lord, Travis. It's not your shame. He forced it on you."

"But I shouldn't have taken you there."

"Not your fault. I practically ordered you to do it." Several minutes passed before she could add, "None of it was your fault. And you did what I asked." As she spoke, she struggled to regain her composure. The new normal, because she didn't think her life going forward would be what anybody considered normal.

It seemed that the children from that clinic had become an obsession for Smith. That, and his utter lack of morality were a terrible combination.

As her mind switched back to a previous snippet of conversation, a bolt of insight shot through her, and she knew Travis felt it.

The children from the clinic.

"What is it? What's wrong?" he asked, catching the weight she put on the words.

"Not...wrong...something amazing."

He made a derisive sound. "Oh yeah?"

She stroked his arm, going back to something she hadn't grasped the import of earlier. "He was talking about your mother having fertility treatments at the Solomon Clinic. About all sorts of far-out stuff that happened when two children from the clinic got together."

Travis nodded.

"Remember when I started to interrupt you when you were talking about your mom's fertility treatments.".

"I'd forgotten...but yeah."

"Well, I think..." She gulped. "I think *that's us.* My mother had fertility treatments, too. She used to throw that at me when she was ranting about me being defective or something. She'd gone to a lot of trouble to have me. She'd even brought me back there a couple of times for testing. And look what an unsatisfactory offspring I was. I didn't have any friends. I was probably on the spectrum. Or worse, like maybe I was going to turn out to be schizophrenic when I got a little older."

Travis swore. "Oh, nice. And I thought my dad was bad. He did have a reason to hate me. I mean, I killed the woman he loved. And he was left with a screaming brat he had to take care of."

"Who would think about their child that way?"

"A man who felt cheated by the way his life had turned out."

Olivia shook her head. "Yeah, we're a real pair. A total disappointment to our parents. But think about the implications." She felt her excitement growing. "I'll bet you any amount of money that our moms went to the same clinic. And now we have an opportunity to catch the guy who strapped you to a table and went at you with an electric drill."

Travis made a dismissive sound. "But I don't know who he is. I don't know where to find him. The only things I know are that he's not Mr. Smith—and he has a fixation on the children from the Solomon Clinic."

Olivia wasn't about to accept the negative assessment. "He thought he was so smart, but he outsmarted himself." It was impossible to tamp down her surge of optimism. "With the powers we're going to develop, I know we can find him. And when we do, we're going to be a lot better equipped to deal with him than we are now."

"What do you mean? How?"

She gave a mirthless laugh. "He *told us* how. He told us about the skills that bonded couples might possess. We're going to see which ones we have and develop them. He ticked off a bunch of paranormal abilities. We already have some of them."

"Like what?"

"To start with—like your being out there somewhere in the darkness and finding me." And then there are the little sparks we created. And the light bulb shattering. We did those things. He gave you a bunch of stuff to try. And maybe there are some he doesn't even know about and can't imagine."

"Not just sparks and light bulbs. We can talk mind to mind."

She could tell by the way he said it that he was getting excited about the possibilities.

"But think about the bigger implication. I mean...you were out in the darkness somewhere, and you found me. Somehow we stopped you from...crossing over or whatever it's called."

She felt his chest heave. "Yeah, somehow out in the darkness—I had a vision of you."

They were both silent for several moments, taking it in.

She turned in his arms, and he held her to him. She felt him trembling, or was that her? Against all odds, they'd accomplished a miracle.

She found his mouth with hers, and they kissed, both marveling that they were together—despite what Smith had done to him.

She was breathing hard when they broke apart. She wanted to take this further, but how far could it go?

Perhaps she was afraid to find out, because she damped down the sexual impulse. They would have time to explore that, but now, they had business to attend to.

His hand tightened on hers. "He gave us a road map. He told me too much because he was sure the only way I was getting out of that room was dead. Even when he tried to fake a connection with that woman he conjured up, he probably knew he couldn't pull it off."

She gave him a triumphant look. "But we're the real deal—with a bunch of possibilities just waiting to be harnessed." She went on, a new sense of power welling inside her. "When two children from the clinic get together, they..." She stopped and turned one palm up.

"They become more than they ever could have been as individuals," he finished for her. "I mean, my being here is proof of that."

"Yes."

Her thoughts switched back to Mr. Smith. "The bastard. He must be a psychopath. But why the hell is he so interested in the children from the clinic?"

"Think about it. If we have powers like that, we're like a walking weapon. For good or evil."

"He talked about couples who died when he threw them together."

"But the way he put it, I got the impression that there are other couples who got together and developed their powers like that detective he mentioned and the woman who was the fiancée of a drug dealer. Didn't he say they got away from him?"

Travis nodded slowly. "You're saying there are other people like us?"

She laughed. "We'll not exactly like us. I think we have something nobody else has."

CHAPTER NINE

Gabe Bowman looked at the addresses Miss Wilder had given him. They were both in St. Stephens, about an hour and a half away. He wanted to begin the investigation. Maybe Carson's house was a logical place to start.

He drove through the flat countryside where corn and soybean fields had once been. There was still some agriculture, but it was now interspersed with shopping centers and townhouse developments, which were the hallmarks of modern life.

Carson's old clapboard house, sitting on a street that dead-ended at a wide creek, wasn't one of them. It had probably been built early in the last century, long before the Bay Bridge made the Eastern Shore more accessible to vacationers and those seeking a slower lifestyle.

The creek thwarted Gabe's plans. He had intended to drive past as though he were looking for another address. But when the water stopped him, he was forced to turn around. As he backed out of a driveway, he spotted a man sitting in a car across the street and several houses down from Carson's place. Gabe kept going, but he knew the guy had taken note of him. It could have been curiosity at seeing a car on this seldom-traveled byway, but Gabe suspected that someone was staking out the house.

Interesting and disturbing. When he'd talked to Miss Wilder, he'd thought that there was going to be an innocuous explanation for Carson's disappearance. Now he wondered if he'd been too quick to make assumptions. What if someone had killed or kidnapped Carson and wanted to make sure nobody found out about it?

Gabe had planned to check out the house and then head for the dock where Carson's boat was moored. Now he decided he'd better take a more circumspect approach to his assignment. At the corner, he turned right and drove several blocks while deciding on how to proceed.

He didn't think it was a coincidence that someone appeared to be watching the house. If he drove to the boat dock and encountered a similar situation, that might decide his next move. But one thing he did know, he was going to be a damn sight more cautious from now on.

OLIVIA LOOKED OUT THE WINDOW, surprised to see how light it was. Their conversation had so absorbed her that she'd lost track of time. She didn't realize how much the night's activities had drained her until she stood up and had to reach for the bedpost to steady herself.

Travis was instantly by her side, "What's wrong?"

"I'm feeling a little dizzy. I think I'd better have something to eat."

"Right."

She gave him a long look, realizing she could see him quite clearly now. Their connection had changed him. He looked...

Like a living man?

His silent thought flashed into her mind, and some of the heady sense of accomplishment she'd been feeling drained away.

Don't forget how all this started, he cautioned.

Right—with his reaching out to her after he'd been murdered, because she knew for sure now what had happened to him.

Feeling as though someone had landed a solid blow in the middle of her chest, she made a quick trip to the bathroom. After using the facilities, she pulled on fresh underwear, sweatpants, and a loose T-shirt. When she looked around for Travis, she didn't see him. Had he withdrawn to recharge or something? Or was he giving her some space again? She decided not to call out to him as she headed downstairs.

In the kitchen, she began looking through the refrigerator. She supposed most people had special foods they ate for breakfast. She preferred leftovers. She'd brought home a creamed potato-and-sausage soup a few days earlier.

Now she pulled it out, ladled some into a mug, and set it in the microwave. While it heated, she retrieved a caramel-flavored coffee pod and inserted it into the machine. The microwave had just signaled that the soup was done when the doorbell rang.

After hearing about Travis's horrendous encounter with Mr. Smith, she couldn't help tensing. But when she peered out the front window, she saw a FedEx driver standing at the door. She'd been expecting a shipment of some acrylic paint, and this must be it.

When she opened the door, the guy said, "I need a signature."

"Of course." She reached for the pad and used the stylus to sign.

"Where are you going to put it?" a voice suddenly asked from behind her.

She whirled, not expecting that Travis had followed her downstairs. She could see him clearly standing in back of her.

"Something wrong?" the delivery man asked, as though he hadn't heard Travis and couldn't see him either.

"No," she managed.

The driver kept his gaze on her. "Uh, you look like you saw a ghost or something."

She made a choking sound. "I guess I'm not feeling well." Quickly, she took the package and closed the door.

When she turned back toward the hall, Travis was still standing there.

"Did you do that on purpose?"

He sighed. "Okay, yeah, I wanted to find out if he could tell I was here."

"Was that all?"

"What else?" he shot back.

"Maybe you wanted to remind me that..." Her voice trailed off when she found herself unwilling to complete the sentence.

He didn't finish the thought for her. Brushing past him, she went back to the kitchen and retrieved the soup, wondering if she could eat it now.

"I'm sorry," Travis said behind her.

"You want me to remember that this isn't exactly a normal relationship."

"I wish it were."

She did too—with all her heart.

"I guess we have to..." She had started to say "settle," but changed it to "be thankful for what we have."

"I am," he agreed. "But is it enough for you? I mean, you have a life. You interact with people who will never be able to see me.

"Are you trying to say this relationship isn't good for me?"

He shrugged.

Wondering why he was suddenly looking on the negative side of things, she said, "Let me be the judge of that."

After adding some half-and-half to her coffee, she brought the mug to the table and sat down.

He took the chair across from her. It was strange to see him sitting there. He should be eating breakfast, too.

I don't need food.

I know, she answered as she sipped some soup.

She had brought her laptop to the table. While she ate, she Googled the Solomon Clinic and found out some interesting information. The place had burned down thirty years ago. And then an explosion at a research facility the doctor was still running killed him and a nurse who had worked at the clinic with him.

Travis followed along as she read. "I'm betting the fire at the clinic wasn't an accident."

"Yeah."

"And what about that later explosion?"

She shrugged. "Sounds like trouble followed him."

"Maybe the government terminated his research—with prejudice."

She winced. "You think they'd do that?"

"Maybe, if it was part of a cover-up."

"Do you think Smith did it?"

"Don't know. But I'm sure he knew what happened."

Although Olivia tried to gather more information, there wasn't much more to learn about Dr. Solomon and his clinic. Finally, she closed the laptop with a sigh. "Dead end."

"But we should figure out what we can do."

"A lot of choices."

"We should start with something easy."

"Which is what?"

"I'm not sure. But it's probably better to go outside before we try hurling any thunderbolts."

"Agreed. And begin by mastering something easier first."

Her gaze fell on the napkin holder at the side of the tabletop. It was one of her own creations, an old wooden box painted with a garden scene. Taking out a napkin, she laid it on the table.

"It's not heavy. Maybe we can make it move."

"How?"

"If we both tried to move it, we'd be fighting each other. Maybe one of us should try to do it, and the other will add...power."

"You do the moving," he suggested.

As she focused on the napkin, she sensed Travis's energy pushing into her. It felt strange, a little like a mild electric current. She kept her gaze on the napkin, willing it to lift from the table, putting her own energy into the attempt, although she wasn't exactly sure what that meant.

For long moments, nothing happened, but she wasn't going to give up so easily. Hadn't Smith been sure they could do this kind of thing?

She felt her muscles tighten as she focused on the napkin, willing something to happen. And then, to her shock—it did. The thin paper lifted off the table, then fell back to the flat surface as though it had been hit by a fleeting air current.

She glanced up at Travis and saw a look of triumph in his eyes. "I'll be damned."

The small success made her redouble her efforts. Now she had a little better idea of what she was doing. As Travis gave her a kind of power assist, she raised the napkin a couple of inches off the table, making it ripple like the motion of a manta ray's fins as it glides through the water. The manta ray image caught Travis's imagination. He grinned at her, and she knew he had taken control of the experiment. Now she was the one lending him energy as he made two edges of the napkin flutter more as it took flight and sailed off the table. She watched in amazement as it flew around the room, picking up speed as it went, circling the table.

"My God," she gasped.

The napkin executed one more circle before coming down for a landing where it had originally been lying.

You didn't think we could do it.

I wanted it to work.

You were the one who suggested we try out some of those things Smith told me about.

I did. But I wasn't sure.

What do you want to try next?

Something harder.

Before Olivia could say what that might be, the phone rang, and she jumped. She'd been so focused on what they were doing that the outside world had gone away. She didn't want to answer, but when she got up and looked at the caller ID, guilt flooded over her, and she snatched up the receiver.

CHAPTER TEN

"Ms. Langston?" a voice asked.

"Yes."

"This is Sarah Riley from Unique Interiors."

The name of the shop was like a stab to Olivia's chest. She'd been so caught up with her unknown ghost and then with Travis that she'd completely forgotten about her business obligations.

"What happened?" The voice on the phone went on. "We were expecting you this morning."

"I know. I'm sorry," she said again. "I got hung up with something. I'll be there as soon as I can."

When she clicked off, she saw Travis watching her. He didn't have to ask what was wrong. He could read it in her mind.

"You were supposed to deliver a bunch of furniture to that shop this morning."

"Yes," and I have to do it. It's too short notice to call

anyone else. Will you be okay if I leave you here for a while?"

He laughed. "As you saw from that FedEx driver, nobody's even going to know I'm here."

"Right."

"Or are you asking if I'll be okay on my own?"

Maybe I was wondering if I'll be.

Before she could say more, he was beside her, turning her to face him and wrapping her in his arms. She closed her eyes, clinging to him, wishing that she hadn't met him, when it was already too late.

He didn't answer her, only held her close, his hands sliding possessively up and down her back, and she knew his thoughts and emotions mirrored her own. She longed to stay in his arms—stay with him, but she had to deal with the real world now.

"I'd better get dressed," she finally whispered.

When he let his arms drop, she eased away from him and headed down the hall. Upstairs, she took a quick shower and pulled on clean jeans and a T-shirt.

"I'd ask if you needed help loading the van, but I can't exactly carry anything," Travis said.

"At least until we get better at moving stuff around with our minds. Then we can fly it from here to there."

"A paper napkin isn't quite the same as a wooden bench."

"Maybe we can get to that point. But luckily for today, the shipment is already in the van. I had a local guy load it for me. All I have to do is drive it over there."

"You're going to St. Stephens," he said abruptly, and she knew he'd pulled that piece of information from her mind.

When she nodded in acknowledgement, he added, "I don't like your going over there."

She'd been trying to put the location out of her mind, but he'd picked it up. It was the town where he'd lived, the town where the kidnappers had chartered his boat. For all he knew, it was also where they'd find Mr. Smith, although he couldn't be sure of that.

"I'll finish my business and come right home," she said, wondering if she was telling the truth, knowing he was wondering the same thing. But there was no point in their discussing it further.

They hugged again before she went outside, and she wanted to cling to him. She wanted to call Sarah and say she couldn't come. Instead, she pointed the van down the driveway. As she increased the distance between herself and Travis, she tried to hold the mental link with him. At first, she could still feel it, but by the time she reached the road, she was alone. More alone than she had been before he'd turned her life upside down.

For Olivia, it was a strange feeling to be disconnected from Travis. At first, she'd felt like he was stalking her. Then when she could finally acknowledge that she welcomed his presence, she'd thrown herself into the relationship. She'd been alone for so long, and suddenly there was this presence who understood what she'd been going through all these years. He'd lived it the same as she had.

Well, not exactly the same, but similar. She'd let herself start to feel that this was the beginning of something normal. But it wasn't. It couldn't be. The rest of the world would never understand the magic of it.

Yet at the same time, it was a relief to be away from him for a while. There was nothing she could hide from him. Every thought, every emotion was open to him. Was there a way to shield her mind? Was that one of the skills Smith hadn't mentioned because there would be no reason for him to know about it? The only things he'd picked up on were outward manifestations of the link between the children from the fertility clinic.

When Olivia got to the Bay Bridge, she had to concentrate on her driving. Like many people who had to cross the bridge, she shuddered over the height and the feeling of being suspended above the water. As she traversed the span, she kept her eyes glued to the car ahead of her, and when she got to Kent Island on the other side, she breathed a little sigh of relief.

From there, it was a straight shot down Route 50 to St. Stephens. Unique Interiors was on Main Street, where most of the tourist-centered businesses were located. She drove around to the parking area in back and went in to find Sarah Riley.

"Sorry I couldn't get here sooner," she apologized the moment she saw the shop owner.

"You're here now. Thanks for coming right over."

Two men were on hand to unload the chests, benches, and tables that Olivia had brought over. She and Sarah inventoried the new arrivals, and Olivia signed a consignment agreement. She could have opted to sell the items to Sarah outright, but that way, she would have had to accept less money. When she took the risk of leaving a consignment, she earned a greater share of the profits.

With the transaction completed, she returned to the van. She'd told Travis that she was coming right back, but even when she'd made the statement, she'd wondered if it was true. In the back of her mind, she'd been planning to stop by the marina where Travis's boat was parked. Maybe she could even slip on board and have a look around. To pick up clues? Or was that going too far? Surely the men who'd abducted him wouldn't have left any evidence. But they could have overlooked something, another part of her mind argued, like...what about fingerprints?

She made a scoffing sound. If people regularly chartered the *Far Horizon*, there would be tons of fingerprints. It would be like trying to locate a particular guest who had stayed in a hotel room.

Still, instead of immediately turning for home, she reached into the seat pocket in back of her and took out a sun hat. After pulling her hair into a ponytail and securing it with a scrunchy, she tucked the gold-red mass under the hat and checked to see if any was showing. She shoved a few loose strands out of sight before turning toward the marina. It wasn't at the main dock in the downtown area, but at a smaller facility on one of the wide creeks that ran through the area.

BEFORE INVESTIGATING Brant's Creek Marina, Gabe stopped at one of the shopping centers that were springing up even in this once remote area. In a sporting goods store, he bought the cheapest fishing rod he could find, along with a tackle box. On surveillance assignments, he always kept a change of clothing in his trunk. He pulled out a pair of well-worn jeans, scuffed athletic shoes, and a plaid shirt. He used a dressing room at the store to change, then added an Orioles cap to the outfit. He debated stopping at a bait store to buy some worms, then decided that it was going too far. Nobody was going to search him for night crawlers.

In his new disguise, he headed for Brant's Creek. As he'd done at the house, he checked out the area. The marina opened onto a parking area that also served several small stores. In fact, if he still wanted bait, he'd be able to get it right here—also coffee, a sandwich, or some sports clothing. Maybe they would have been cheaper than at the more modern-looking place where he'd shopped.

As he cruised past the shopping area, he spotted a guy in a green shirt slouched down behind the wheel of a battered Ford. His face was hidden by the bill of a black baseball cap. Although seeing the guy wasn't ironclad confirmation that the area was being watched, it was suspicious, particularly since Gabe had been sure that someone was staking out Carson's residence.

He drove past, noting that instead of a sidewalk on the

creek side of the street, there was a six-foot-wide board-walk with a sign announcing the marina. Coming off the boardwalk at right angles were five narrow piers with boats moored on either side. Some were quite small, but others were probably the right size for the *Far Horizon*.

Miss Wilder had told him that Carson's boat was moored along the second pier from the left. He couldn't see the vessel from the street, but it couldn't be too far away since the creek was narrow.

He drove past and pulled into a space at the edge of the parking area. He sat there for twenty minutes, watching to see if the man in the car had any obvious reason to be there, but the guy stayed where he was.

Gabe cursed under his breath. If he got out of his car and headed for the boat, he could be putting a target on his back. He debated leaving and coming back by water. But the watchers might have that end covered as well.

He was about to leave when he saw a white van come slowly by. A woman was at the wheel, and he watched her circle the lot, looking for a space. She could be making a delivery to one of the boats or one of the stores.

As he watched her, he had the feeling that she wasn't familiar with the area. There was no reason to believe he should keep an eye on her, but just in case, he jotted down the license number of the van as she circled past again, then found a space and parked.

She didn't get out immediately, but when she finally made a decision, she stood staring at the marina sign as though she were psyching herself up to approach. Her hesitation gave him the opportunity to get a better look at her. She was slender and very appealing, dressed in jeans and a T-shirt, and wearing a wide-brimmed hat that didn't quite match the outfit. An attempt to disguise her appearance? He thought she was probably in her late twenties or early thirties, with the pale skin that probably belonged to a redhead.

Was she somehow connected to the men who had abducted Carson? Or was she here for the same reason as he—trying to find out what had happened to him?

There was no solid reason to make assumptions about why she was there. But he'd learned to pay attention to his hunches. Now her indecisive behavior solidified his feeling that she wasn't planning to buy fishing tackle. Was she here because of Travis Carson? And if so, where did her loyalties lie? With him, or the mysterious men who were staking out his house and marina?

When she finally made up her mind to head for the marina, Gabe saw the slouching guy sit up and take notice.

The woman hesitated for a moment before angling toward the second pier from the left—the one with Carson's boat.

Grabbing his fishing pole and tackle box, Gabe strode across the street. He let her get onto the boards of the dock. Before she had taken more than a few steps, he made it onto the boards.

"Honey, wait up!"

She turned, confusion plastered across her face.

"This is the wrong marina," he called out, loud enough for Mr. Slouch to hear.

"I don't..."

Before she could finish, he added in a much lower voice, "There's a guy in the parking lot watching Travis Carson's boat."

The look of shock that bloomed confirmed his suspicion. She'd been heading for the *Far Horizon*. And she wasn't in league with the watchers.

"We have to go down to the Main Street dock," he continued, taking her arm and leading her away from the water. "That's where we're supposed to meet our charter."

She allowed herself to be led along for a few moments before trying to jerk her arm away. He held firm.

"He's watching. Bend your head. I think he's going to take our picture."

"Who's watching?"

"A guy in a dark green T-shirt, black baseball cap, jeans. He was here when I arrived." When she tried to look, Gabe held her back. "Don't."

Emotions chased themselves across her face. "How do I know...?" She stopped and started again. "Who are you?"

"I could ask the same questions."

As they talked, he led her to the far side of her van so that Mr. Slouch's view was blocked.

In the shade of the vehicle, she raised her head and asked, "Who are you?"

"I was hired by Carson's aunt to find out what happened to him."

"What's her name?"

"Lydia Wilder."

"Why should I trust you? You could be one of the men who killed him."

The moment the words were out of her mouth, her skin went white, and her features turned sick.

"Killed him? You think he's dead? What do you know?" He was tempted to grab her and shake her, but if Mr. Slouch came around the side of the van and saw, that wouldn't jibe with the story he'd been working hard to establish.

She made a moaning sound. Panic flashed in her eyes. "I...don't know...anything. Let me go."

A bolt of satisfaction shot through Gabe. Maybe he was finally getting somewhere.

CHAPTER ELEVEN

Olivia yanked open the van's door and then slammed it shut, making sure to click the locks. The man who had accosted her on the pier had to jump out of the way as she started the engine and barreled out of the parking lot.

When she looked behind her, she saw him standing next to where the van had been and holding a fishing rod like a flagpole. She also saw a man in a dark green T-shirt and an Orioles cap, which kept her from getting a good look at his face.

Her heart was pounding, and she wanted to press the accelerator to the floorboard, but she kept her speed under the town limit as she headed for the Bay Bridge. Travis had warned her not to go poking around his boat. And he'd been right.

She filled the car with curses. She hadn't listened to him, and now...well, she didn't exactly know what now.

"Shit. Shit. Shit." She hadn't even gotten Fishing Pole's

name. She should have, so she could check him out. In their brief encounter, it had seemed like he was trying to protect her. Or maybe that was a ruse to get her to trust him.

At least he hadn't gotten her name, either. Could he find it out? And what about the guy who Fishing Pole had said was staking out the marina? That could be true, or it could be part of the fake scenario. She bashed her palms against the steering wheel. She hadn't handled that right at all. But she hadn't been expecting anyone else to show up at the marina. Maybe she should have.

Still feeling like her insides were being churned around in a washing machine, she headed for home.

GABE HURRIED BACK to his car, threw his fishing gear inside, and headed after the van, hoping that the guy from the parking lot thought they were just going to meet up again at the town dock.

He was tempted to follow her and find out where she was going. But he didn't have to do that. He had her license plate. As he drove away from the marina, he glanced in his rearview mirror. Mr. Slouch was not following. Probably he had orders to stay in position, but had he phoned someone to pick up Gabe's tail?

He drove around several streets until he was sure he didn't see anything suspicious. Then he went back to the shopping center lot and called Decorah Security. Teddy

Granada, one of their IT guys, ran the plate for him. The van belonged to Olivia Langston, and the picture on the driver's license Teddy sent him matched the woman he'd just met.

He spent the next three-quarters of an hour on his laptop, researching information about Olivia Langston. She was an artist with the unusual occupation of creating custom-painted furniture. Probably she used the van for delivering custom pieces to clients.

She lived in Frederick. Had she crossed paths with Travis Carson? She'd blurted out that he was dead. How could she know what had happened to him unless she was involved?

OLIVIA MADE for the safety of home. She should never have gone to the marina. She should have just delivered the furniture to Sarah and left.

Now she had to face Travis, and he would know immediately what had happened.

Again, she cursed her own stupidity. But it was done now, and she couldn't take it back.

She saw him the moment she stepped into the house. He was in the front hall standing as though he'd been waiting there for her the whole time she was gone. He looked as solid as she had ever seen him—and like a man whose wife was hours late coming home.

There was no way he could miss the look of worry on

her face. He started to say, "What's..." but stalled in mid-question, and she knew he had pulled the recent scene at the marina from her mind.

She felt a wave of emotion rolling off him, a mixture of fear, confusion, and...anger. He had told her to stay away from his boat, and she had tried to do just the opposite. Only she had never gotten there.

"Sorry," she breathed, starting to shake. When she reached to wrap her own arms around her body, he got there first, pulling her to himself and holding her. Lord, it was wonderful to feel those arms around her. As she had gotten used to doing, she closed her eyes, making him all the more solid.

His hands stroked comfortingly up and down her arms. He was silent as she sensed him mentally reviewing what had happened.

"Do you have an Aunt Lydia Wilder?" she whispered against his chest.

"Yes."

That brought a small measure of relief. The guy hadn't been lying about that part. "And she'd be worried about you? I mean, enough to hire a detective?"

"Yeah, sometimes it felt like she was the only one who cared about me."

"So she might have hired that guy to find out what happened to you."

"She's very precise. She would have done some research and picked a top agency."

"I could call her..."

"And make the same mistake again?" he asked sharply.

She felt her face heat and burrowed further into him. "Right. How do I know you?" She thought for a moment. "I suppose I could make up some story about booking you for a charter, and you weren't there when I got to the marina."

"That sounds kind of lame. And how would you know to call her? You'd have to be closer to me than a fishing charter customer."

"Right."

"Let's not get her any more tangled up in this."

She knew part of his decision came from worry about his aunt. "Okay."

And she knew he was reviewing her memories, seeing the scene from her perspective. In a voice she couldn't quite hold steady, she asked, "Was the guy who said he was a detective one of the men who kidnapped you?"

"No. So he could be telling the truth about what he was doing there. What about the other guy?"

"You didn't get a good look at him, but I don't think it's one of them."

"I guess Mr. Smith probably has more men working for him."

Travis eased away from her and started to pace up and down the hall. The mixture of emotions she had first seen on his face had solidified into worry.

"You think Smith sent the other guy to watch the marina?" she asked.

"I do," he said in a flat voice, then added, "Too bad we

don't know the detective's name. I'd like to warn him to watch his back." He raised his head, his gaze locking with hers. "You could be in danger."

A frisson went down her spine. "Nobody followed me. I don't have a sign on my van or anything."

"Let's hope there's no way to connect you." He stopped pacing and turned to her. "We need to be able to protect you. Hurling napkins at Smith's men isn't gonna cut it. Let's go out and try some of those fireballs he mentioned."

She glanced toward the window. "It's light out there."

He laughed. "A fireball will show up a lot better in the dark." He followed her gaze. "This is a pretty big property, and there are a lot of trees between you and the road."

"My parents planted them for privacy."

"And we've got it. Nobody is going to see what we're doing up here."

She nodded. "Fireballs," she mused. "How are we going to work it? Conditions have been pretty dry here. I wouldn't want to start a blaze."

"Let's set something up in the driveway, like target practice."

She thought for a moment. I have a metal step stool. We could put..."

"Tin cans on it," he supplied.

Now that he had suggested something positive to do, she felt better. Hurrying to the pantry closet, she retrieved the step stool along with a grocery bag with empty cans ready for recycling.

From behind her, he said, "I wish I could help you."

"You *are* going to help me by giving me the power to do it."

She took the step stool outside and set it on the blacktop about ten yards from her workshop. When it was in place, she opened the recycling bin and fished out several cans. "They're not going to burn."

After setting one of the cans on the stool, she surveyed the arrangement. "I guess we should aim perpendicular to my workshop. We don't want to set *that* on fire."

"I'm thinking that a shot isn't going to go wild. We'll be focusing on the can," he said.

Nevertheless, they also faced away from the house. Olivia backed up almost to the front windows, and Travis moved in behind her, pulling her into a close embrace, so that his body almost felt like it was part of her.

"I think you have to generate the attack," he murmured. "I'll give you power like we did with the napkins."

She narrowed her eyes, focusing on the can, not sure exactly what she was supposed to do. Then she thought about a battle she'd seen in a space opera movie. As the ships fought each other, beams of light shot out from each ship toward the other. She struggled to summon something similar—a beam of destruction that would damage the can.

Good, Travis approved.

She felt him pouring energy into her, and as he did, she kept her imaginary beam on the can.

Sweat broke out on her forehead as she tried to create

some kind of ruinous attack on the innocent can that had held diced tomatoes. At first, nothing happened. In frustration, she willed her mind to produce the effect she wanted. And suddenly it happened, almost like a death ray striking the can. It started to glow, then leaped up into the air. Thinking it might explode, she pressed her hands over her face until she felt the can clatter to the blacktop.

"I think we did it," she marveled as she hurried over to the ruined vessel. It lay on its side, the exterior charred and the metal partially melted.

Wow, Travis gasped. *I guess Smith was right.*

Let's try again.

Don't touch the can.

I won't. She got a rake and pushed the target out of the way before setting another on the stool.

I need to be able to do it, too, Travis said. *Let me see if I can direct the power.*

So we should reverse our positions.

She moved to his back and clasped her hands around his waist.

From his position behind a tree, Gabe surveyed what he could only think of as the Langston estate. There was a wide lawn leading down a gentle slope to a wood lot that gave him cover.

The house occupying pride of place at the top of the hill was probably a couple of hundred years old, but the exterior was freshly painted. In back and to the side was what he took to be an old carriage house, converted into a garage and probably converted again into her studio. The woman he'd encountered in St. Stephens must be doing pretty well with her painted furniture, even if she had inherited the property from her parents.

He'd picked up that information from one of the articles he found about her—both in the local Frederick paper and in a couple of art magazines. He'd had his phone read them to him on the way over. He knew a lot about her background and her artistic talents, but he still had no idea why she'd been recklessly heading for Carson's boat. And then there was that intriguing line about "one of the men who killed him."

As he moved from tree to tree, getting closer to the house, he saw her come outside carrying a two-step metal stool, the kind that was dangerous to use because there was nothing to hang onto when you stepped on top.

She set it in the driveway several yards from the house and the workshop. Once it was in place, she opened a plastic grocery bag she was carrying and pulled out a can that had probably held some tomato product, judging from the red color. After taking several steps back, she stood oddly, and he would have sworn that someone was behind her, holding on to her, but there was no one else in the scene. She stood still, her focus on the can. As far as he could tell, her arms remained at her side, and her eyes were locked on the can. From the look of intense concentration on her face, it seemed like she was putting considerable effort into something—focusing mental energy on some difficult task.

For long moments, nothing happened, but then it looked like a beam of light shot out from...somewhere...and struck the can. It started to glow, then leaped into the air like a jolt of electricity had struck it. As it shot upward, she pressed her hands to her face, looking shocked that anything had happened. In the next moment, the can clattered to the blacktop.

Jesus! What the hell was that?

He watched her get a rake and push the can out of the

way, before pulling another one from the grocery bag and setting it on the step stool and moving back to where she'd been stationed earlier. Only this time her stance was completely different. There was no one standing in front of her, yet her arms were raised in a circle at waist height as though she had locked them around another person. But there was nobody out here besides her and Gabe. Even stranger, she leaned to the side as though she had to look around the person she was holding to see the can.

What the hell? He stepped out from behind the tree to get a better look at whatever weird scenario was being played out.

The same attitude of concentration was on her face, until it was replaced suddenly by a look of shock and alarm.

"No, don't," she shouted.

Seconds later something struck Gabe in the solar plexus. He doubled over, and as he went down, he blacked out.

"TRAVIS, WHAT HAVE YOU DONE?" Olivia shouted as she ran toward the man who was lying on the ground. As she got closer, she saw that it was the guy from St. Stephens who'd said he was a detective.

She could feel Travis behind her as she dropped to her knees beside the fallen man. His eyes were closed, his face was deathly white, and his breath was shallow.

I spotted him...sneaking up on us. I just reacted.

You might have killed him—or," she lifted one shoulder. "Or worse," she added aloud.

"When you screamed, you pulled back your power, and I did too. I think I just stunned him."

"Hopefully. But we can't leave him out here." She gave the supine figure a long look. "Unfortunately, I don't think I can get him to the house by myself."

"Maybe I can help."

"How?"

"Lift his shoulders. I'll do his feet."

"You can do that?"

"I think so, now that we've done that trick with the fireballs."

She bent to take the unconscious man by the shoulders. At the same time, his feet and legs lifted. Travis took more of the weight, and it was like the two of them were carrying the guy. Still, it was a struggle to get up the hill. Luckily, Olivia had left the kitchen door open, so that they didn't have to put down their burden when they got to the house. They carried him into the living room and laid him on the modern sectional sofa that she had bought when she'd redecorated the house.

Olivia went to get a blanket, and by the time she was back, their visitor was looking more normal.

"Maybe he just needs to sleep," she said, as she covered him with a blanket.

"I mean, I hope we don't have to call a doctor. What would we say happened to him?"

"Yeah," Travis muttered. "Sorry."

"You thought we were under attack."

"Getting abducted and killed can make you jumpy."

"I understand." She was about to back away from their victim when she changed her mind. "He probably has a wallet. Maybe we can find out who he is."

She had just reached into his pocket when iron-hard fingers wrapped around her wrist. At the same time, another hand came up and aimed a pistol at her face.

Olivia gasped and tried to back away.

From behind her, Travis shouted, but she was the only one who heard it.

"What did you do to me?" he growled.

"Nothing."

"I saw what you did to the can. Then you did it to me."

"Let me go, and we can talk."

"Why should I trust you?"

"I brought you inside. I could have left you out there on the ground."

"So nobody would see me."

"If I thought someone was going to see, I wouldn't have been doing the thing with the cans."

He thought about that for a moment before saying, "Fair enough."

When he let go of her wrist, she backed away.

"Why were you digging in my pocket?"

"To get your wallet and find out who you are."

"Gabe Bowman," he snapped, then winced. "Again, what the hell did you do to me?"

What do we do? She asked Travis.

I made a mess of this by hitting him.

She could feel him mentally sighing. *Maybe we have to tell him some version of the truth.*

Like he's going to believe it.

If we do it right, it might work.

"Why are you just standing there looking like you're going into a trance?" Bowman demanded.

"It's complicated."

He slowly sat up. "You got any aspirin? Or anything else for the bitch of a headache you gave me?"

"I didn't," she reiterated.

"Then what hit me?"

Without answering, she said, "I've got some NSAIDs. Let me get you a couple of pills and a glass of water."

"So you can think up a good story?"

"So I can figure out how to tell you the truth so you'll believe it."

When he scowled at her, she turned toward the kitchen. She was back in a few minutes with a bottle of pills and a glass of water.

She took a seat in a chair opposite the sofa, and Travis sat on the other end of the couch where she could see both him and Bowman.

"Spit it out," he ordered.

She and Travis had been silently conferring while she got the water and the analgesic.

"I'm going to back up a little," she began.

Bowman watched her closely.

"You know how scientific experiments can go off the rails." Without waiting for an answer, she went on. "About thirty years ago there was a doctor in Louisiana who'd convinced some government special projects agency that he could create super-intelligent children by manipulating blastocytes soon after fertilization. He was running a fertility clinic, which was where he got the genetic material to work on."

The detective pulled out a notebook and ballpoint. "What was his name?"

"Douglas Solomon. His contract with the mothers specified that they bring the children back for IQ testing periodically. Not all of them complied. When he did the tests, the kids had a normal intelligence spread, and the think tank that had paid for the program shut down the clinic. Right after that, it burned. And more recently, a lab Solomon was running exploded. Sounds suspicious, right?"

The detective winced.

Olivia hurried on. "We can talk about the clinic later. The important point right now is that there was something unusual about the children after all."

Her gaze flitted to Travis before she looked down at her hands. "None of them was able to form close relationships with anyone—until they came in contact with another child who was born out of Dr. Solomon's experiments." She looked up again. "When they did, one of two things happened. Either they formed a psychic connection, or their brains couldn't take the strain, and they died of cerebral hemorrhage."

Bowman shifted in his seat. "A psychic connection? Like what?"

"They could do things like read each other's minds— or, uh, make fireballs and use them as weapons."

There was dead silence in the room while Bowman processed that information.

"You don't believe me?" Olivia asked.

"I..."

"You got hit by one. Luckily, we're not too good at it yet."

"We? I only saw you. Doing...something." He stopped short and fixed her with a steady gaze. "Wait a minute. You and who else? Travis Carson? You said he was murdered."

"Unfortunately. But somehow he found me and came back."

"You expect me to believe that?"

She shrugged. "Can you give me another explanation for what happened to you? Maybe I'm up here developing a death ray when I'm not painting furniture?"

Bowman kept his gaze steady. "You're saying that Travis is dead and you brought him back?"

"No—he was drawn to me, and he came back. Because we're both children from the Solomon clinic."

"So he's a ghost."

"I wouldn't use that term."

"What term would you use?"

"I'm not sure. I just know that we bonded. Somehow I kept him from..." She spread her hands. "From crossing over to the Other Side, or whatever you want to call it."

"Jesus Christ. Give me a break. You expect me to believe that cockamamie explanation of why you assaulted me?"

She dragged in a breath and let it out. "I was pretty sure you wouldn't. But when you woke up on the sofa, you asked what I'd hit you with. I wasn't the one who did it. It was Travis. He saw you sneaking up on me, and he was afraid I was going to get kidnapped and killed, too. He attacked you with something you'd call paranormal."

Bowman stared at her. "If any of that's true, where is Travis now?"

"He's sitting on the other end of the sofa—wishing he could join the conversation. Unfortunately, I'm the only one who can hear him or see him."

The detective's head swiveled in that direction. "You're saying you see him now?"

"Yes."

His eyes hardened as he looked around the room. "I don't see anything."

"As I said, he can only...manifest to me."

He swore again, but his expression turned inward. "Maybe you picked the right person to tell this story to."

"What do you mean?"

"I work for an outfit called Decorah Security. We've got a lot of agents who have powers nobody would believe unless they saw them for themselves."

"Like what?"

"Like stuff I can't tell you because I'd be breaking confidences. But I will say that we've got a telepath in the group. And other guys who could get jobs in a superhero movie. Only they wouldn't be faking it."

She stared at him. "So you're at least willing to withhold judgment on my being crazy—or a liar."

"Yeah. But ..."

"But what?"

"You've got to admit that bringing somebody back from the dead is a pretty far...bridge."

Her voice faltered a little. "Bringing him back from the dead isn't exactly accurate. As you said, you can't see or hear him. He isn't actually back, not in the normal sense." She laughed. "Normal, right?"

Bowman nodded, his brow furrowed.

"How about a demonstration of the power we have together? I mean, besides his hurling a thunderbolt at you."

"Like what?"

She glanced at Travis, and they held a quick, silent conversation before settling on a tactic. Without warning and without her moving from her seat, they snatched the pen out of Bowman's hand.

He made a startled sound, then caught his breath as the pen stayed in the air and flew around the room. It landed with a small thump on the lamp table beside the sofa.

Bowman looked at Olivia and shook his head. "That was a nice trick, but maybe it's like the mediums who put on a show for the customers they're fooling."

"Is that what you really think?" she shot back. "They

probably do their tricks with elaborate setups. I didn't have any prep before I got your pen."

"I guess so," he said slowly. "But it doesn't prove that Travis Carson is here."

"He's sitting there looking pretty frustrated. I'm worried that he's going to give you another energy jolt."

"I thought he couldn't do it by himself."

"Fair point. But he might make a Herculean effort for you."

She was trying to decide what to do next when Travis leaped up and came around behind her chair. Reaching for the ends of her hair he lifted them up then moved his hands so that the hair looked like it was dancing.

"Stop," Olivia ordered.

He did as she asked, then came up in back of Bowman, which would have been impossible if he'd had any physical substance. He lowered his fingers to the detective's scalp and began to move them like bugs creeping across the man's scalp, only harder.

Bowman sucked in a sharp breath.

"You can feel that?" Olivia asked.

"Yes, like my scalp's crawling," he said, his voice not quite steady. Lifting his head, he said, "Stop."

When Travis lifted his hands and resumed his place on the sofa, their guest asked, "Tell me what you want from me."

CHAPTER THIRTEEN

Harold Goddard, alias Mr. Smith, had sent men to watch Carson's house and the entrance to the marina where he kept his boat. The watcher at the residence had noted that the same car had driven past a couple of times. The guy had been able to snap a photograph of the driver. He looked to be in his late twenties or early thirties, but it wasn't possible to pick up much detail from a photo of a moving car. When he froze and enlarged the image, he only got a picture of a guy with a ball cap pulled low. And the camera hadn't captured the license plate.

The man watching the dock hadn't noticed any unusual activity, but Harold had also been able to set up a camera on a telephone pole at the edge of the parking area. Now he scrolled through the tapes, looking for the same car—and found either it or its twin, a Chevy Blazer. This time the driver was a guy wearing casual clothing and carrying a tackle box and a fishing rod. He looked like he was on his way to a fishing trip. But that could just be a disguise designed to throw off anyone watching.

Interestingly, he caught up with a casually dressed young woman who was also heading for the dock. Stopping her before she entered the marina, he steered her back toward the parking lot, where they disappeared behind a white van.

They were there for several minutes, after which they both pulled away—the van first.

What was going on here? On the face of it, they looked like they had planned to meet up at the dock. And then? She'd shown up at the wrong marina, and he'd told her where they were really supposed to be. Or what? Had the guy who had driven past the house earlier come to the dock dressed in fishing gear so anyone watching would assume he was there for recreational purposes? Then he'd seen the woman and told her what?

Was he surprised to find her there? If so, how did he know her? Was she a friend of Carson? In Harold's research on the man, he hadn't come upon anything more than casual liaisons with women.

He didn't like it. Too bad he didn't have the license plate of the van, either. But was there some other way to figure out who she was? At the very least, he'd have to instruct his men watching the house and the marina to look out for both suspicious vehicles—and suspicious individuals.

GABE KEPT his gaze on Olivia Langston.

"What do we want from you? The same thing Travis's aunt wants, only we're a couple of steps ahead of her. A guy who called himself Mr. Smith captured Travis, tortured him for information, and then killed him."

Still coping with the concept of the ghost, Gabe asked, "Travis told you that?"

"Of course—Travis. Who else would know?"

"Motive?"

"He was either working with Dr. Solomon or knew about his experiments. He's obsessed with the children from the clinic. He's tried to capture them before, but because they were bonded, they got away. So he changed his tactics and went after a lone individual—Travis."

"Why does he care about the children?"

She shrugged. "I believe he thinks we'd be useful. Or dangerous."

Gabe considered that. If you had to make sense of this weird situation, that might be it.

Olivia began to speak again. "We were trying to figure out how to find Mr. Smith and make sure he doesn't do this to anyone else."

"Like you?" he said pointedly.

She winced. "Me and anyone else he might go after. You were already trying to figure out what happened to Travis. We can help each other."

As she spoke, Gabe thought he heard the echo of a male voice under Olivia's. What? Was he getting sensitized to the ghost?

He hardened his expression and punched out his words. "First, let's get some things straight. You've already found out that Smith is totally ruthless. He kidnapped, tortured, and killed an innocent man. To make sure nobody goes after him, he has operatives watching his victim's boat and also his residence. If you want my help, you have to promise me that you're not going to do any more investigating on your own. I mean, you don't want to end up in Smith's torture chamber, being asked to explain how you know anything about Travis Carson, do you?"

He was glad to see a flash of fear cross her face as reality set in.

"I guess not."

"You guess? If I wasn't clear before, I'll say it again. Stay away from the guy and let me do my job."

He started to stand, but his legs buckled, and he landed back on the couch. So much for the hard-ass detective who was going to take over from the amateurs. Currently, he didn't have the strength to get up.

Olivia gave him an apologetic look. "It looks like that thunderbolt has aftereffects." She shook her head. "We were just starting to practice it, and we didn't know what it would do."

"Maybe I'm lucky you were just getting into it." He dragged in a breath and let it out. "Okay, I'm going to see how much work I can get done here. Bring me my laptop from the car."

"I could lend you a laptop."

"No. I've got access to databases you don't. The car is

parked in a little turnoff along the road. Turn left when you get to the end of your driveway." He fumbled in his pocket for the key and handed it to her.

"Do you need anything? More water?"

"That would be good, but get the laptop first."

When she left the room, he turned his head to the other end of the sofa where she'd said Travis was sitting. "Are you still here?"

Nobody answered, but the piece of paper on the table moved a little as though it had been ruffled by a sudden gust of wind.

"Do me a favor and clear out. I don't like the feeling of someone watching over my shoulder while I work."

There was no audible reply, but he hoped the ghost was considerate enough to respect his wishes.

The ghost. He was thinking of Travis Carson as "the ghost."

He thought again that Olivia Langston had run into the right detective down at the dock. How many people would be willing to accept her ghost explanation? He had an advantage because of his friends at Decorah Security. Hell, some of them were werewolves. And one, Hunter Kelley, had even been the victim of a rogue government experiment. He hadn't even had a name until Katherine Kelley had been hired to socialize him because he was a clone being raised for a suicide mission, and the men training him didn't want to think of him as a human being. To them, he'd just been a tool until she'd rescued him.

So Gabe understood about illegal, overreaching

government projects. He closed his eyes and leaned his head against the sofa back. If he wasn't careful, he was going to fall asleep. Probably he did, because the next thing he remembered was Olivia putting down his glass of water on the table.

When his eyes snapped open, she handed him the laptop and turned to leave. Maybe the ghost had told her Gabe wanted to be alone.

"Thanks." He drank some of the water and set the glass down before picking up the laptop. Then he got into one of the databases he'd told her about. It had information on under-the-table government projects. He found nothing in them on the Solomon Clinic, which wasn't exactly a surprise. But he was also able to search local newspaper articles.

There was one about Dr. Douglas Solomon opening his clinic in Houma, Louisiana, a little over thirty years ago. Then there wasn't anything about it until the story of the fire that destroyed the property. Because it occurred at night, no one had been hurt. All that squared with what Olivia had told him. The local fire inspector had given the cause as a gas leak.

That might have been the end of the story, but as Olivia had suggested, the doctor didn't shut off his activities with the destruction of his clinic. He'd kept working at a lab built on the property owned by one of his former nurses. Both of them died when *that* facility blew up in an explosion just a year earlier. Gabe wondered what the guy had been fooling with when his second facility went up.

But reading about the fire and the explosion wasn't going to get him any closer to locating Smith.

He looked around the room, then said aloud, "Carson, I know I told you to leave, but I'm wondering if you could give me some help."

Again, the paper on the table lifted, making the hair on the back of Gabe's neck prickle.

"Maybe I can ask you some questions," Gabe went on. He looked at the paper that had moved of its own accord. "How about you make the paper flutter twice for yes and once for no?"

He held his breath until he saw the paper lift before settling back on the table.

"Okay. Do you think there's anything in your house that would help me find Smith?"

The paper lifted once before settling again.

"And on the boat?"

This time, there were three flutters.

"That means you don't know?"

Two flutters.

Gabe sighed, then asked, "Are you tied to this house? I mean, can you go anywhere else?"

The question was answered from the doorway as Olivia stepped into the room. Her gaze flitted from him to the other end of the sofa and back again, and Gabe assumed she was looking at the ghost.

He hadn't had a chance to get a good look at her before. Now he took in her riot of long wavy hair, her pale skin, her delicate features. He couldn't help thinking that if she was in a relationship with a ghost, she was wasting her affection.

He clenched his teeth, hoping that she couldn't read minds. He had no business thinking anything personal about her, but he hadn't been able to stifle the thought.

Pulling his mind back to business, he asked, "When I went down to St. Stephens, I could feel the connection with Travis fading. By the time I reached the road, I couldn't sense him anymore."

"But maybe it's possible to change that. Why would he be tied to this house? He didn't know you before Smith...went after him," he finished,

"That's right."

"You said Smith talked about all kinds of powers that the children from the Solomon clinic had. Hurling thunderbolts. Moving objects with their minds. Smith probably didn't know all they could do."

"I think he was also afraid they could read minds," Olivia added.

"But he has no idea as to the extent of their powers. Maybe it's different for different couples."

She nodded before crossing the room and taking the chair where she'd been sitting earlier.

"Why don't you and Carson...?"

She interrupted. "He'd like you to call him Travis, if we're going to be working together."

"Okay, yeah, Travis."

"Can we call you Gabe?" she asked.

"Of course." He cleared his throat. "Why don't the two

of you try to…" He stopped and flapped his arm. "I don't quite know how to say it, but you said you and Travis, um, bonded. I'm hoping there might be some way he could come along with you when you leave the house."

"So you've bought into my crazy story about Travis finding me after Smith killed him?"

"Yeah. I guess I have to."

She looked excited, and the paper on the table fluttered.

Then her eyes narrowed. "Not exactly a ringing endorsement."

"You have to admit, it's a hard claim to sell." Gabe pushed himself up. "But I like it. It would be very useful to have an unseen presence who could perform psychic *tricks*."

"And do what? You told me to stay away from St. Stephens."

He sighed. "I know, but now I'm rethinking. Travis would be protection for you that Smith couldn't possibly expect. Why don't the two of you see what you can do?"

"Like what?"

"Like deepen the bond between you so he can go wherever you go."

He pushed himself up and was glad to see that he was feeling almost normal when he stood. Maybe he had come up with a whole new approach to the case, but he cautioned himself not to get too excited. Maybe he'd asked Olivia and Travis to do what was impossible

CHAPTER FOURTEEN

"Where are you going?" Olivia asked.

"First, do a little more research. Then I need to get another car. I have to assume that the guys watching Travis's house will be on the lookout for my current one."

"How long will you be gone?"

"Why don't we meet back here tomorrow morning? Meanwhile, I'll be in Beltsville."

"Why Beltsville?"

"That's where the Decorah Security office is located." He reached into a pocket and pulled out a business card, which he set on the end table. "If you need to reach me, the number is on here. The phones are manned 24/7."

"Okay." She cleared her throat. "What if we can't do what you asked?"

"I'll have to come up with something else," he answered.

The words weren't reassuring.

When he left, both Travis and Olivia stood, stumbling toward each other and meeting in the middle of the room. Perhaps they hadn't realized the kind of tension they'd been under. It had started when Travis knocked the detective unconscious, and had continued during their desperate maneuvers to get him to believe their wild story. Now that they were alone, the strain of the past few hours came crashing down around them.

When he reached for her, she flung herself into his embrace. As he pulled her close, she molded her body to his.

They clung together, relief flooding through them. The detective had bought their story—then gone off to do some prep. Alone at last, they held onto each other, rocking slightly, each leaning onto the other for support.

Olivia marveled at how mortal the man in her arms felt. With her eyes closed, she had the perfect illusion that he was as legitimate as anyone else. More so—to her.

He walked her backwards, maneuvering her around the table, and taking her down to the sofa so that she lay on her back, still with her eyes closed so as not to break the spell. Her body had turned molten, and she knew Travis could feel it. When she raised her face, he lowered his head and his lips came down hard on hers, then softened as he began to kiss her with the same urgency she felt. And he had the advantage that he could reach the back of her body as easily as he could the front. His hands stroked up and down her back and clasped her bottom, pulling her more tightly against himself.

When his hands moved to her front, caressing her breasts, she felt her heat level shoot up. She wasn't undressed. He had to be touching her through two layers of fabric, her bra and her T-shirt, but it was like he was caressing her naked skin. He found her hardened nipples, stroking across them in a maddening rhythm that turned her center liquid. When he took them between his thumbs and fingers, she gasped in need.

"I want ..."

"I know."

One hand slipped under her jeans, stroking through the slick folds of her sex, coming up to find her point of greatest sensation, then sliding down again to press against her entrance. Two fingers slipped inside, and she felt herself clench around him. He pushed in and out of her, while the heel of his hand pressed against her center, and she was helpless to do anything but move against him. He held her to him, keeping her grounded as she came undone in a blaze of sensation that shuddered through her whole body and made her struggle for oxygen.

She clung to him, eyes still closed, coming back to earth.

What he'd given her had been glorious. More than she had ever expected in her life. Yet she couldn't help craving more. She didn't say it, but she knew he picked up her thoughts.

"I'm sorry," she whispered.

"It is what it is," he answered.

"But we're going to change the parameters," she

vowed. "Deepen our bond so you can come with me when I leave."

Inside her head, she heard him make a snorting sound. "Damned if I know how."

Ignoring the obvious, she pressed on. "We're going to try something that none of the other couples needed to do, even if we don't quite know how. But think about it. Yesterday, we didn't know how to pick up a piece of paper without touching it. Or make a thunderbolt, or whatever you want to call them."

"But we were trying for some kind of physical effect. This is different. I'm not...physical."

They were both silent for long moments, contemplating the detective's request.

Travis had said he didn't know how to accomplish it, but he was the one who suggested, "Let's start with—I was out in the darkness, and I was drawn to you. Getting to you should have been impossible, but somehow, we accomplished it."

"You're the one who did it," she pointed out. "Somehow you connected to me when I wasn't expecting it, when I was afraid of it." She dragged in a breath and let it out.

"And now that we've gotten this far, we can both try to make this new thing happen."

She could even see that as logical.

"So, how do we make it so you can come along with me?" As she spoke, he moved aside so she could sit up.

Let's start with something familiar—let's find out how far I can get from you and still feel our—bond.

Good idea. She stood and walked out of the room without looking back, trying to keep the connection going.

We've got more space to maneuver if we're outside, he said.

Changing course, she walked through the front door and dragged in a lungful of the cooler evening air.

When she looked back, she saw Travis standing by the door. She turned again and walked down the driveway toward the road. At first, she felt his presence as strongly as if she'd been standing beside him. But after about fifteen feet, she could sense the bond weakening. She focused, trying to make the connection come back to full strength, but she couldn't figure out a way to do it.

They spent several frustrating minutes trying to get the effect they wanted, each of them mentally reaching for the other, but she simply didn't know how to make it happen.

Finally, she walked back and pressed her shoulder to his. "When we did the other stuff, we were touching—one of us giving the other energy."

But I think we have to do this without touching. What if you try to forge a deeper link, and I lend you power?

Okay.

Once again, she put distance between them, walking to the limit of where she could feel him faintly in her mind. Sweat broke out on her body as she struggled to bring him into sharper focus. No matter how much she tried to invite him to join with her, it had no effect.

Switch roles, his faint voice suggested. *I was the one who reached out to you first.*

Yes. She let him take control, reaching out to draw her to him. As he did, she fed him energy. Again, it had no effect.

Exhausted, she staggered back to the patio and plopped into a chair. "So much for our awesome abilities," she muttered.

She sat with her head bowed, breathing hard, trying not to feel like she'd been doing a tremendous amount of physical labor. Whether she fed him power or they reversed their roles, it didn't seem to make any difference.

Frustration bubbled inside her, and she made one last desperate attempt to pull him toward her in a way that would keep him there. But she simply couldn't do it.

Tears leaked from her eyes, and she struggled to hold them back, but she knew Travis felt her sense of failure. He had found her when it should have been impossible for them to connect. And since then, they had done some amazing things together. But this even more intimate link seemed as likely as spinning wisps of cloud into silk.

She tried to think about it logically—if you could apply logic to such a seemingly outlandish situation. Travis was the one who had found her. She had to be the one to cement his attachment to her, but she simply couldn't figure out a way to do it.

He stood behind her, rubbing her shoulder, and she knew he could feel the tension that tied her muscles into knots. She had been putting everything into this new effort, and it had gotten her nowhere. She glanced around and was shocked to see that it was pitch black now. She'd been at this for hours, and she simply didn't have the energy to continue.

"He'll come here tomorrow, and I'll have to tell him we couldn't do it."

He wasn't expecting any help from you when he took the assignment. He didn't even know that you existed.

"He didn't know what he was up against. We may be the only thing that can keep him from ending up in Smith's torture chamber—and then the bay."

She felt Travis shudder as though he were reliving what had happened to him—and then absorbing the enormity of the task ahead.

Still, his silent voice was calm as he said, *You can't keep pushing yourself like this. You need to eat something and then get some rest.*

I'm not hungry.

You need food if you're going to continue. You're not going to accomplish anything in the state you're in. You have to recharge. Eat something and then lie down for a while.

His words made sense. Almost too tired to move, she heaved herself up and shuffled into the kitchen. When she opened the refrigerator, she found several cartons of food she'd ordered. Pulling one out at random, she stuck in a fork and ate some. It was cold, and she didn't even know what it was, but she shoveled in a little more.

When she'd eaten all she could stomach, she shoved

the carton back into the fridge. As she closed the door, she struggled to stand, swaying on her feet. If Travis hadn't been there to wrap an arm around her waist, she might have toppled over. Instead, she let him lead her out of the kitchen. She looked at the stairs, thinking she didn't want to expend the energy to climb them.

You can lie down on the sofa again.

She didn't argue when he steered her toward the den, where she flopped down. She felt him ease down beside her where there shouldn't have been room for him.

Perhaps she slept. She wasn't sure. She woke when he stirred beside her, then felt him tense. "What's wrong?"

I was thinking about when Smith said to me, when he was trying to get information, when he was telling me stuff about the children from the clinic.

She drew in a quick breath, remembering the horror of his telling.

The bastard gave away a lot because he thought there wasn't going to be anyone I could tell.

She nodded against his shoulder.

Something just flickered into my mind.

She felt his excitement.

He said *there was a sexual component.*

The observation made something in her memory click. "Wait—didn't we first make those sparks after..."

Right. After I brought you to climax, he finished for her. *And what if I turned you on again, and kept you that way? No telling how much we could do.*

You think sexual...need could...be the key?

There's nothing to lose by trying it.

She heard a chuckle in his voice as he said the last part. Wrapping his arms around her, he shifted their positions so that she was lying sprawled on top of him.

"Let's see how it works." As he spoke, his hands stroked over her back and downward to her bottom. His fingers cupped and stroked, and the fatigue she had been feeling vanished—replaced by heat building inside herself. She wanted to squirm against him, but she managed to stay still while he did things no other man had ever done. He knew just what pressure would turn her nipples into aching points of sensation because he felt everything she was feeling. He worshiped her breasts with his hands, then his mouth, suction making her back arch. He kept two hands on her breasts while another hand worked its way down her body.

She stopped worrying about how that could be possible as his fingers dipped into her, then slid upward through her slick folds to her center.

When she tried to rock her hips against him, another hand held her in place.

She moaned, "I need to come," she gasped out.

"And you will. When we're ready."

She wanted to plead that she had never been more ready, but he kept up the maddening conquest of her body —a conquest that would have been impossible for any other man.

His voice murmured in her ear, inside her head. *That's right...let yourself revel in it.* With anyone else, she might have been embarrassed at how totally she was in his power. With Travis, she allowed herself to sink deeper into the sorcery of the moment. He kept up his total conquest, making her whole body quiver with need. Need for him. Need for completion.

Not yet. We're not there yet, he crooned. *Reach for me. Pull me in.*

How do you know what to do? she gasped out.

Because when I was lost, I pulled myself toward you.

She understood then. He had tied himself to her. It wasn't exactly the same, but he had managed to forge a link between them. Her breath came in gasps as she reached out for something she didn't know how to capture.

It's all right. I didn't know what I was doing when I went looking for you. But it worked. You'll figure this out, he encouraged her.

As he spoke inside her mind, she realized what she had to do. She had to want it enough, like he had wanted it enough when he'd found her, like he had overcome any hint of failure. Bonding to her like that had been monumental all by itself. But if he could do it, so could she.

Not you, we, he corrected. *We can only do it together.*

Yes! She clung to all of it—to his words, to his needs. To her own need.

A tiny sliver of fear wormed its way into her mind. She knew if she accomplished this joining, she would never be the same again.

She pushed that doubt away. Never be the same? That was a good thing. If she managed this seemingly impossible task, she would never be alone again. The man who made love so ardently to her now had been lost to himself. But somehow he had reached for her—and found himself again. If their resolve and their courage held, they could do so much more. Together.

Banishing any shred of doubt, she focused on what he was doing to her, what they were doing together. The tension inside her burst in a great spasm of pleasure, an orgasm that consumed her as no physical sensation ever had in her life. And as she came, she felt his penis, hard and thick inside her, where she had wanted it since the moment he had touched her.

The wonder of it overwhelmed her as she felt his orgasm too, pounding through him—through both of them.

She cried out aloud, shouting her pleasure and her triumph to the world. His arms tightened around her as his harsh gasp of wonder joined hers. They had joined together as no other humans ever had in the history of the world. He was with her. Inside her in a way that was like a miracle.

They came back to earth together, both of them hardly able to believe what had happened. She felt his body as well as her own. The joining created a confusion of sensations, which they struggled to sort through.

I went along with it, but I didn't really think it was possible, she marveled.

I wasn't going to let you give up.

But now what? What can we do together?

I guess we'll find out. He laughed, a sound of wonder

and joy. *And then there are the interesting sexual possibilities.*

She flushed, remembering him touching her everywhere at once, and then the feel of him inside her.

He rolled to his side, taking her with him, and they lay together as she struggled to regulate her body. After he shifted their positions, neither of them moved for long moments, and in the aftermath of the tremendous exertion, she drifted off to sleep.

She wasn't sure how much later she woke with Travis's voice in her head. *He's coming.*

Her eyes flew open. "What?"

Gabe is coming up the walk.

"Oh Lord, how do I look? Or can you see how I look?"

Yes.

"How?"

She felt his mental shrug. *Satisfied.*

Embarrassment flooded her.

Maybe only I can see it.

Or maybe not.

Do I look...different?

To me.

Like what?

Too new to describe.

I wish we had more time to figure stuff out.

For all we know, Smith could be planning to move away from the area. We have to strike while we can.

She had been focused on her newfound intimacy with Travis. Now his words sent a jolt of alarm through her.

The last thing she wanted on earth was for Smith to get away. She wanted him to pay for what he had done. And before he died, she wanted him to know that he hadn't wiped Travis Carson from the face of the earth. He was here now, with her, ready to do what he had to.

The doorbell chimed, and she jumped up. She wanted to stop in the bathroom, pull herself together, and look at her face in the mirror. Did she look transformed? Did she look like she'd just had the mother of all orgasms? Teeth clenched, she rushed down the hall and pulled open the door, then stood staring at the man standing on the front porch.

"Gabe?"

"Yeah."

The character who had rung the bell didn't look like the one who'd left the house the day before. Was that only yesterday? It felt like a lifetime.

"What time is it?" she asked.

"Five."

Her eyes slid over him. He must be wearing a wig because he now had long, light brown hair caught in a ponytail in the back. He had on a ratty green T-shirt and jeans with holes at the knees, and his sneakers looked like they'd been dragged through mudflats. When she looked at them, he kicked them off onto the porch.

Her gaze rose again. Somehow, he'd changed the shape of his face. Maybe he'd put something in his mouth to pad it out. And his nose was larger and redder.

"I wouldn't recognize you."

"That was the idea. Now we'll see what we can do about you." As he spoke, he hefted the gym bag he was carrying.

"What's that?"

"The outfit you're going to wear."

"Okay."

He gave her a speculative look and asked, "Did it work?"

She didn't have to ask what he meant, and she couldn't prevent heat from creeping into her face. "Yes."

"How did you do it?"

She felt her flush deepen.

Her reaction brought a bit of color to his complexion as well. "Okay, sorry I asked."

Needing to change the subject, she looked out the door and saw a beat-up, ten-year-old Chevy that went with the character he'd transformed himself into.

Her gaze must have turned skeptical because he said, "It's got a powerful engine under the rusted hood."

"Okay."

Still feeling awkward, she stepped aside to let him in. She might have taken him to the couch, except that a picture of herself and Travis in sexual ecstasy sprang to her mind, and she had to pivot quickly away. Glad her back was still turned, she headed for the kitchen and glanced around as though she were seeing the familiar room for the first time.

"Uh, coffee?" she asked.

"If you're having some."

"I am." She didn't really need any caffeine, but getting the fixings gave her something to do besides awkwardly confronting him.

"I've got lots of pods. What do you want?"

"No fancy flavors."

"Kona okay?"

"Sure."

As she and Gabe talked, she was vividly aware of Travis observing the interaction in amusement.

I'm not gonna brag about our exploits, if you don't.

Gabe's casual answer was a nice counterpoint to her awkwardness.

"Maybe I shouldn't have come so early," he said, his gaze flicking over her.

"No, it's okay."

She made the first mug for him. "You want anything in it?"

"Black is fine."

When the machine had made her serving, she added cream to her mug, pulled out a chair, and sat at the table.

"So how does it work?" he asked. "What does it mean that he's with you?"

She shrugged, feeling awkward again. Now she had two new relationships she never could have imagined. With Travis she had an unbelievable intimacy which she wasn't going to try to describe to Gabe or anyone else. And with Gabe she had a kind of unintended intimacy. He knew the secret of her bonding with Travis. And he believed her.

But it was more than that. She knew he was attracted to her, and she realized that somehow her bonding with Travis made her more open to him as well. If that made any sense.

Deliberately letting the observation go, she focused on his question. "I don't know how to describe it. I feel him with me."

Putting it politely, Travis chimed in.

Stop it. This is hard enough without your making editorial comments.

Gabe was speaking again. "Can he move away from you?"

"I don't know. You woke me up. We haven't tried anything fancy yet."

As she spoke, she was aware of Travis's silent laugh. *That wasn't fancy enough for you?*

CHAPTER FIFTEEN

"Let's find out," Gabe suggested.

"Okay."

Olivia felt Travis step a few feet away. She saw him, but more dimly than he'd been manifesting to her before their crazy transformation.

As he walked several feet farther, she began to feel a tug or a strain. When he took another step, she called out, "Stop."

He went still.

"Did you feel that?" she asked.

Yes. It was unpleasant.

Right.

"What's the answer?" Gabe asked, barging into the silent conversation.

"At the moment, about twelve feet. But we can probably make that farther if we practice."

"Um, maybe you should." He paused before saying, "I

asked you to do this so that Travis can help me capture one of the men who's staking out his house. And I'd like you farther away when we do it."

"You belong to the school of—the guys do the dangerous stuff and the womenfolk hide in the bushes?"

He shot her a sharp look. "Look, you know what he did to Travis. What do you think he'd do if he had a woman in his clutches?"

Olivia winced. She didn't like the answer, but it made sense. She felt a little chill sweep over her as she remembered Travis's description of his own interrogation and murder.

"Okay, we'll see how far apart we can get," she said. "Make yourself comfortable, and we'll go outside."

Gabe looked like he wanted to say, "Don't take too long," but he only pressed his lips together.

She took another sip of coffee, then exited through the kitchen door, and Travis stepped through the wall. It seemed that the new physical connection between them hadn't affected his ghostly status.

They headed for the patio, where she lowered herself into one of the chairs. Travis paced to the edge of the flagstones before stepping off into the grass. They weren't quite to the limit of their bond yet, and he took a cautious step forward. Again, she felt the uncomfortable sensation that she might have described as insects crawling over her skin, only it was also inside her body.

She shuddered.

Yeah, he agreed.

Interesting that he didn't have a body, but he could feel it.

"Let's change places," she said.

He might have asked why, but he didn't need to. Whatever she was thinking was fully accessible to him.

"I wonder if there's some way to shield my mind to keep you from reading me like an e-mail. Maybe that's another skill we have to practice."

It's probably easier when the two people are more separated, he finished.

As she got up, he returned to the patio and stood with his arms crossed, watching her.

She reached the spot where he'd had to stop and felt the unpleasant tingle again. This time, she strove to banish it by bringing back the memory of the two of them on the couch, when he'd kept her at a peak of sexual need until there was nothing else she could do but succumb. The heat the memory generated helped to dissipate the creepy-crawly sensation.

Inconvenient to have to turn yourself on to get away from me, he quipped.

She answered with a small sound. "Don't pull me out of the moment by making me feel ridiculous."

Sorry.

The technique seemed to work, and she was able to double the distance. The sound of the door opening startled her. She expected that it would have made the effect snap off, but she didn't feel the discomfort.

Gabe was standing on the patio, looking from her to

where Travis was standing. "I was watching out the window," he explained.

"You can see Travis?"

"Not exactly. But I kind of see a disturbance in the air."

"Let's hope nobody else can."

"I think they might—but only if they'd spent some time with him." He shifted his weight from one foot to the other. "Do you think you could push the distance any farther?"

"Maybe, but we'd have to keep practicing."

"This may be far enough. You should change, and then we'll leave."

They went back inside, where Gabe took her outfit from the gym bag. It included a dark wig and an industrial-looking outfit with the logo of a well-known big-box store. Probably she was supposed to be a checker or one of the workers who restocked the shelves.

"I'll go up to change," she said. She also intended to take a shower because the activities of the night and the previous day had made her sweaty. Upstairs, she quickly cleaned up before changing into the clothing, which fit her pretty well. It was a little hard getting all her hair up under the dark wig, but she managed it with a rubber band and a bunch of hairpins. When she was finished, she could see that the dark wig gave her a very different appearance, although it was a bit startling in contrast to her pale skin. Deciding that a grocery checker would want to look her best, she put on a little lipstick and blusher.

Examining herself critically in the mirror, she decided that it would be hard to recognize her. She and Gabe now looked nothing like the couple who had been at the dock yesterday.

When she came downstairs, Gabe gave her a critical inspection. "Good job," he approved.

"You picked out the outfit."

"And you look perfectly comfortable wearing it."

She glanced at Travis, *So what did you two talk about while I was gone?*

We haven't reached that stage in our relationship yet.

"I've started recognizing when I'm being left out of a conversation," Gabe interjected.

"I was just wondering if you two were talking about me while I was gone."

"You're kidding, right?"

"Only half."

Olivia climbed into the passenger seat of Gabe's clunker. He slid behind the wheel, and Travis settled in the back seat.

When they were on the road to the Bay Bridge, Olivia asked, "What's the plan?"

"First, we see some of Smith's guys watching Travis's house or the marina. The house would be best, since there will be fewer people around on that dead-end street. When we locate them, you'll stay out of sight. Then Travis will get their attention with a horror movie thing so I can make a capture and run an interrogation."

"He wants to know—what kind of horror movie thing?"

"Anything paranormal that will scare the crap out of them so I can get them under my control and ask some questions about where to find Smith."

"Okay," Olivia answered. She didn't love the scenario, but she knew Travis was looking forward to some payback.

It was a two-hour drive to St. Stephens from Frederick. On the way they discussed tactics that they might use, but Gabe cautioned that they couldn't come up with a plan until they encountered the actual situation.

Olivia could feel her heart start to pound when they reached the St. Stephens town limits. She knew Travis was picking up on her reaction when he said, *You'll be out of the line of fire.*

I don't want to be. You know I want to help.

The best way you can help me is by my knowing you're safe.

She sighed. *Okay.*

Gabe turned onto the street where Travis's house was located. As he drove past, he said, "Keep an eye out for a car with two men sitting inside—last time it was a five-year-old Chevy. But it could be something different.

Travis spotted the watcher, and Olivia conveyed the information to Gabe. *He's in a Range Rover.*

"I see it."

Travis uttered a curse that only Olivia could hear. *What?*

There's only one guy. But it's one of the men who abducted me from the boat. The one named Pete.

Oh Lord. In a shaky voice, Olivia gave Gabe the news.

"That's good," he answered.

"How is it good?"

"We know he's in contact with Smith."

He's looking at us, Travis said. "It's only him, as far as I can tell. Not the others."

"I'm going to turn onto the next block," Gabe answered. When he reached the corner, he executed the maneuver and pulled down several car lengths along the curb so that he was no longer in the line of sight of the watcher.

As the vehicle came to a stop, Olivia felt like she was hanging on to a wire with electricity coursing through it.

Gabe turned his head to look at the backyards of the houses along the street. "Some of them have fences," he reported. "But there's an alley. Slight change of disguise. Pull the logo off your shirt, and we'll switch it out for the electric company."

"Why didn't we do this in the first place?"

"Because it was a fifty-fifty proposition that we were going to end up at the dock, where you could have been on your lunch break or something. But this is a better setup. Now you need a disguise that will give you a reason for being *here.*"

He retrieved his bag from the back seat and rummaged inside, coming out with a lanyard that held a name tag. On it was a pretty good picture of Olivia with her dark hair.

"How did you get that?" she asked, as she slipped it over her head.

"Combination of Photoshop and AI. You walk up

through the alley. If anyone asks, you're checking the electric lines.

"What lines?"

"I don't know, but this meter is going to register something that looks official." He pressed a button on the device that activated a blinking red light.

He turned to Travis. "You and I will walk up the sidewalk, keeping pace with Olivia. You can do that, right?"

"He says, yes," Olivia relayed.

"I'll stop at the house before the car and turn in at the walk. You keep going. When you get to the car, do something that will scare the shit out of the guy inside."

He looked back the way they'd come. "Did you see anyone on the street?"

"No," Olivia answered, speaking for herself and Travis.

"Let's hope we don't alarm any bystanders. If they see what's going down, they might call the cops."

Olivia made a low sound. "Now you tell me."

"Probably not gonna happen. Just be alert."

Gabe looked toward the back seat. "Can you open the door of your house?"

"He thinks so," Olivia relayed.

"Okay. We're going to take Pete inside where we can question him in private."

Hoping she could pull off the plan, Olivia stepped out of the car and stiffened her legs.

She waited until Travis and Gabe were on the street they'd come from before starting down the alley. She could feel the connection between herself and Travis stretching almost to the breaking point. What would happen if they got too far away? Would he vanish?"

I guess we'll find out, he answered.

She kept walking, worried that at any time this could all fall apart. But her only option was to keep going.

Can you pick it up a little? Gabe is going to draw their attention at his pace.

At any pace, she shot back before speeding up.

Travis told her when she was behind his house. As she studied the exterior, she was relieved to see that the patch of lawn between his property and the neighbor on the right was not obstructed. She cut partway through and stopped behind a large, unwieldy juniper.

You should have trimmed this monster, but it makes a convenient hiding place now, she said. From where she stood, she could watch the action on the street, but was pretty sure she wouldn't be spotted. She could see Gabe stop, well back from the target car, but she knew he was visible to the man behind the wheel.

The thug looked up, now more aware of his surroundings than he had been a few minutes earlier.

Gabe held his ground, but as she looked on, she heard Travis say, *Give me energy.*

She did as he asked, sending power to him. He waited a moment before charging toward the car and throwing himself violently against the side. The blow made the vehicle rock. It kept rocking as Travis moved his hands against it, and she continued to give him the power he needed. She could feel his elation as he rained some payback on one of the men who had delivered him to Smith.

From her hiding place, she could see panic and confusion bloom on Pete's face.

CHAPTER SIXTEEN

Olivia watched the man under attack check to see if the car doors were locked. They were, but that didn't make any difference to Travis. He pulled the driver's door open and bent inside, pressing himself against the hapless Pete, turning the tables on him. He'd kidnapped Travis, but he was now the captive.

Olivia watched terror suffuse the man's face as he struggled to draw in a breath. Raising his hands, he clawed at the air. When that failed to dislodge the invisible body pressing down on him, he squirmed out from under Travis and flung himself out of the car and onto the grass, where he stumbled and went down. But Gabe moved in quickly, caught him under the arms, and pulled him up. As Pete struggled to get away, Gabe dragged him toward Travis's house.

The three of them disappeared inside, and Olivia ran

to the door, slipping in after them and closing it behind her.

Travis checked the captive's body for weapons. *He's got a shoulder holster and a knife strapped to his ankle,* he said. Olivia relayed the information to Gabe, who relieved the thug of the weapons.

He looked toward Olivia. "I didn't want you to come in here."

"I wasn't gonna stay hiding in the bushes."

"Even though that was the better plan?" Gabe's hands clenched, but he abruptly changed subjects. "Okay. Make yourself useful. Bring me a kitchen chair." When she started off, he called out, "Wait," and gave her a pair of rubber gloves. "You don't want anyone to figure out you were here." As he spoke, he was putting on gloves of his own. He also went to the front door and pulled out a rag to wipe the interior and exterior knobs before turning the lock.

Olivia hadn't even thought of fingerprints. But he was right. It would be a mistake to leave any.

She looked around, located the kitchen, and stepped inside to a fifties breakfast set with aluminum tubing frames and plastic seats and back cushions. Probably they'd belonged to Travis's father, and the son hadn't bothered to replace them.

Okay, so I don't care about style, he acknowledged as she brought a chair back to Gabe.

Gabe pushed Pete into the seat, securing his hands

behind his back with handcuffs, and using rope to tie him to the chair and secure his feet to the chair legs.

The man looked on, wide-eyed, his gaze swinging from Gabe to Olivia.

"You can't do this to me."

When neither of them answered, he went on in a shaky voice, "What's this about? How did you pull off that trick at the car?"

"Professional secret," Gabe shot back.

"Hey, wait a minute," the dirtbag answered. "I didn't do nothin','"

"You were one of the men who abducted Travis Carson from his boat."

"No."

"You're lying."

"No," the man said again, his voice weaker.

Gabe beckoned to Olivia and spoke in a whisper. "We'd better have a lookout. Can you tell Travis to go outside and watch for anyone coming here?"

"Why should they?" she asked.

"I'm not taking any chances."

She looked toward Travis, *I guess you'd better do it.*

She could see he didn't want to leave the scene of the interrogation, but he did as asked, stepping through the front wall.

Gabe filled a pitcher of water at the kitchen sink and brought it back, before pulling a thick towel from his bag.

Pete watched wide-eyed.

"You know what I'm going to do, right?" Gabe said.

"Yeah, and it's illegal."

"So is kidnapping. So is murder. Who hired you?"

As Pete pressed his lips together, Gabe shrugged. "Have it your way."

He pulled out a large piece of plastic sheeting and spread it on the floor before tipping Pete's chair back so that he was now lying on his back. The man's eyes, filled with panic.

"Who are you working for?"

"If I tell you anything, he'll kill me."

"You may not live long enough for that," Gabe answered.

Olivia was watching the proceedings with a kind of sick fascination. She hadn't known what to expect, but it wasn't *this*.

Gabe slapped the towel on the man's face.

"No wait," he begged

"Who are you working for?"

"Smith. His name is Smith," came the muffled answer from under the towel.

"We know that's not his real name. Who is he really?"

"That's the handle he used with me."

"Let's see if you're telling the truth." Gabe poured some of the water from the pitcher onto the towel, where it plastered the covering to the man's face.

Pete sputtered and gasped. "No, please..."

Gabe stopped pouring the water. "If you don't know his name, what *can* you tell me?"

"He lives in a big house. He's got a lot of property. The place backs onto a river."

"You took Carson there?"

"Yes," the kidnapper gasped out.

"What was the name on the mailbox?"

"There wasn't any. Maybe he gets his mail at a P.O. box."

"House number?"

"Maybe there was one, but I didn't pay any attention."

Gabe cursed under his breath, obviously trying to figure out what useful information he could get out of this guy.

He was lifting the pitcher again when Travis came charging back through the wall.

"What?" Olivia asked in alarm.

Two SUVs just pulled up.

How did they find us?

Don't know. But you gotta split, now.

Olivia put her hand on Gabe's shoulder. "Uh, our friend says we have to go. We have company."

* * *

"SHIT." Gabe looked at their prisoner, wishing he'd been prepared for reinforcements to show up. But there was no use beating himself up for what he couldn't change. "Let's go."

He pulled the towel off Pete's head and delivered a

solid blow to his face. His eyes closed, and blood began to leak from his nose.

"Our friend says we have to hurry. They're getting out of the SUV."

Gabe stuffed the wet towel back into his bag, glancing around at the rest of the mess. At least he'd made sure there were no fingerprints.

He grabbed his bag. "Come on."

They ran for the back door, and had just stepped out and closed it when he heard a splintering noise.

He didn't need Travis to tell him that Smith's goons were bashing in the front door.

He and Olivia sprinted down the alley, and he supposed the ghost was with them, seeing as he couldn't get far from her.

Gabe put on a burst of speed, plowing ahead so that he had the car running when Olivia got to the vehicle.

Seconds later, she slid into the front seat and slammed the door behind her. He jerked the clunker away from the curb without waiting for her to fasten her seat belt.

"Travis says they see us," she gasped out the information to Gabe as he barreled down the street.

"I was afraid of that." Looking in the rearview mirror, he spotted a man taking pictures of the car.

From the passenger seat, Olivia asked, "How did they know we were here and where we'd taken Pete?"

"They must have a surveillance system in addition to stationing someone on site." As he spoke, he turned onto the next street. "Or maybe it's worse. Maybe they had Pete sitting in that car to lure us over so they could catch us on camera and swoop in."

"Oh great." Olivia swiveled around. "They're on our tail. They're going to catch up."

And start shooting? Would they risk that in a populated area?

Gabe had the feeling they'd take any risk to find out who was on to their kidnapping and murder game.

They had him blocked in from behind. All he could do was keep driving, executing a series of turns that he hoped would get them in the clear. Instead, he found himself on another street that dead-ended at a creek.

They were trapped.

CHAPTER SEVENTEEN

Gabe briefly considered shooting it out with the bad guys. But no telling how many of them were in those two vehicles, since the windows were tinted. And no telling who else might get hurt.

Looking left and right, Gabe saw there was maybe enough leeway between the creek and the house whose property abutted it for his vehicle to squeeze through.

With no other option, he turned left, forcing the car into the narrow strip of lawn that was barely wide enough for a donkey cart. He took out some kind of bush next to the house. And the wheels on the right side almost went over the bank, but he somehow made it to the next street, where there was a development of townhouses and small tract homes.

One of the boxy little units had an open, empty garage, and he drove inside. Leaping out of the car, he ran to the garage door and slammed it shut.

"What if the homeowner comes in here with a gun?" Olivia gasped.

"Let's hope he doesn't."

He moved to the row of windows, waiting as an SUV sped past. It turned around and came back, slowly inspecting the street. Gabe prayed the driver wouldn't get out and start opening garage doors. When the car finally disappeared from sight, he let out a sigh of relief.

"What's happening?" Olivia asked from the car.

"They're gone, but we'd better wait for a while before leaving."

After half an hour, he decided it was safe to split. All the way back to Olivia's house, he cursed himself for trying this plan. But he'd been desperate. He wasn't going to find Smith without information, and his ploy probably would have panned out, given enough time to work Pete over.

Too bad he hadn't figured on an alternate surveillance system. Still, there was one important piece of information he'd ascertained. The rescue team had arrived quickly, which meant that Smith's base of operation couldn't be too far away.

So, what next? Use a compass to draw a circle on a map and check every house within the radius?

Well, maybe it wasn't that bad. They weren't looking for any of the new little houses around here, or anything in town, for that matter. Pete had said that Smith lived on a big estate on a river. There were a lot of them, but not an overwhelming amount.

"What are you thinking?" Olivia asked.

"About how to find Smith—and how to keep you safe."

"He doesn't know who I am."

"Let's hope not." He gave her a quick glance. He hadn't known her long, but he knew some important things about her. She was courageous and reckless, and he'd quickly come to care about her. He cleared his throat, "But just in case, maybe you should move out of the house until we resolve this."

"No. Where would I go?"

"Where you'd be out of danger."

"No," she repeated. "Travis wants to help you find Smith, and he can't stick around without me."

Gabe had the feeling there was no way to make her understand just how dangerous a game this was. Smith had no compunctions about murdering anybody who could compromise him.

He sighed. "Okay, then you're going to have me as a house guest, because I'm not going to leave you unguarded."

She nodded. "That will give us more of a chance to brainstorm."

HAROLD GODDARD, alias Mr. Smith, looked at the sorry individual slumped in the chair on the other side of his desk.

Pete Roka sat with an ice-filled compress pressed to his nose.

"Tell me again, how did the detective get the drop on you?"

Pete shifted in his seat. "I don't know exactly. The car started to, you know, rock."

"No, I don't know," Harold said, punching out the words.

The man he was interrogating dragged in a breath and let it out. "It was weird, man. The car started rocking, like..." He shrugged. "Like somebody had thrown themselves against it."

Harold felt his eyebrows rise. "Like somebody. But you saw no one."

"No. Just the detective standing a few yards away, watching."

He tried to bring the scene into focus. It sounded like the guy had known what was going to happen, and he was waiting.

"Then the door opened," Roka said.

"You hadn't locked the doors?"

"I did. I'm sure." The words came out like a whine.

"So how did they open?"

Roka's look was pleading. "I dunno. And then it was like somebody pulled me out."

Harold kept his expression neutral as he ran over possibilities in his mind.

The detective had been professional and methodical. Harold's men had gone over the interior of the house. The only fingerprints were Carson's. And the car that looked like a junker had been quite fast. It had led his men on a merry chase.

But it hadn't been fast enough to get so far ahead that Timbers would have lost it. Bowman must have found a place to hide and waited until the coast was clear before making his getaway.

The whole incident was a puzzle. It felt like a combination of careful planning and magic.

Harold made a snorting sound. He didn't believe in magic, although he did believe that the children from the Solomon Clinic had powers.

But he knew the detective wasn't one of them. Harold had checked the rolls. He wasn't listed. Or what if he was one of the ones who had somehow slipped away? No, that wasn't possible. Some of the mothers had failed to take the children back for testing, and their names had fallen off the list. But the Howell Institute had maintained meticulous records of all the mothers and children, even the ones who broke their contracts. And Harold had been working from their list, not the one from the Solomon clinic.

So either the detective was using some kind of magic tricks that Harold couldn't imagine. Or...

What if the woman was one of the children? What if she'd met Carson before his death?

Harold's fists clenched. He had surveilled the man for months. He hadn't gotten together with any women.

Dismissing that possibility, Harold went back to another option. What if Carson had been lying about being able to do stuff on his own? What if it was possible, and he'd somehow been able to hide it?

Harold didn't think so. Not after what he'd done to the man. Everybody broke under torture, and if Carson had known something, he would have given it up to make the pain stop.

But now perhaps the woman was the key.

On the chair in front of him, Roka shifted.

Harold's gaze flicked back to him. He'd like to kill the idiot, but this might be the wrong time for bodies to keep piling up. He couldn't just terminate someone when they were no longer of use to him. He kept a room on the basement level where operatives might sleep if they were on duty here.

"Go down to the dorm," he said. "Get some rest. We can continue this later."

Harold bit back a smirk as relief flooded Roka's face. The man practically sprang from the chair as he headed toward the door, wincing as he juggled the ice pack against his nose.

When he was gone, Harold turned back to his computer. At first, the woman had stayed out of sight behind a large bush. But when Bowman had taken Roka into the house, she'd come out of hiding and joined him. Which was good because he'd gotten some good shots of her face.

He'd fed it into a powerful facial recognition program, and he had high hopes that it would reveal her identity. If he knew who the woman was, he could scoop her up and get back to some intensive interrogation.

OLIVIA FELT a sense of relief when she got back to the house, stepped inside, and locked the door.

The solace evaporated as she watched Gabe walking around, checking locks on doors and windows, even the ones upstairs.

Travis stood behind her, his arms around her waist, holding her tightly. *I hate putting you in danger.*

Not your fault, she answered.

She looked up as Gabe rejoined her in the den. "You don't think they're going to come here, do you?" she asked. "I mean, they don't know who I am."

"I hope not. Are you sure you're not willing to go to a friend's house or something?"

She wasn't going to tell him that she didn't have any real friends. She imagined it was the same for all of the children produced from Dr. Solomon's experiments.

All she could do was reiterate her previous "no."

"Do you know how to use a gun?" the detective asked.

Travis's grip on her tightened as she answered, "My father made sure I did, because this house is in an isolated location. I have a gun in a lockbox here. But really, I'm probably better off using the powers Gabe and I have."

"Maybe not if someone's shooting at you," Gabe

muttered. He had brought in an arsenal, including an automatic rifle.

We need to get better at hurling thunderbolts, Travis said.

She turned to Gabe, "Travis and I are going outside to practice blowing things up."

When his eyes widened, she clarified. "Not literally. But we're going to amplify what we can do."

"If you go out, I'm going too."

When she headed for the door, he picked up the automatic rifle and followed, settling into one of the lawn chairs to stand guard.

FROM HIS COMFORTABLE LAWN CHAIR, Gabe watched Olivia and Travis at their strange weapons practice. It was like nothing he had ever witnessed in his life. There were no actual weapons. All the force of the attack seemed to come from Olivia's body, although logically, Travis must be an equal partner.

Gabe could see when Olivia set up a can on the step stool they were using. Other times, it would look like a can was floating to the stand, only Gabe knew that Travis was carrying it. Once a can was in place, Olivia would face it. He could only see her, but from her stance, he could tell that Travis was also there, either holding her or being held by her, as he was the one launching the power bolt.

Gabe couldn't help imagine the intimate contact, the

natural way Olivia fit against Travis. They must be completely comfortable with each other. More than that, they must have a warm, satisfying relationship—whatever that would be with a ghost.

As Gabe watched Olivia's graceful movements, he found himself contemplating what it would be like to be intimate with her. When he realized he was mentally putting himself into the role of her partner and her lover, he brought himself up short.

Don't even think about it, he warned himself. She was bonded with Travis. She'd said she'd never been close to anyone before the ghost. There was no way another guy— one who wasn't a result of Dr. Solomon's experiment—was going to horn in on that relationship.

It was just a damn shame that she couldn't have a normal sex life. Or could she? What was it that she and the ghost did together?

His gaze cut to her, knowing Travis was nearby and hoping the ghost couldn't read the thoughts of the man who was watching them with envy.

OLIVIA AND TRAVIS kept up the practice as long as they could, trying different variations. Usually, they stood together. Sometimes they tried it several yards apart. And they also kept increasing their distance from the target until it was simply too far for a bolt to hit the can.

After a couple of hours, Olivia could see that their strikes were losing power.

The effort had exhausted her, and she could tell that Travis was flagging, too.

Were they going to defeat the purpose by burning out?

"Maybe we're overdoing it," she finally said.

From where he sat watching them, Gabe voiced his agreement. "You look like you've reached the point of diminishing returns," he said. "Pack it in now, and you can see how it goes tomorrow."

"Okay," she agreed, silently admitting that she welcomed a reason to stop.

SURPRISINGLY QUICKLY, Harold's facial recognition program hit pay dirt, partly because he was limiting his search area to Maryland and Delaware, the most likely places where Gabe's little helper might reside.

It turned out she was Olivia Langston, and of all things, she was an artist who painted furniture—which was carried in some of the shops in St. Stephens. Maybe she'd run into Carson on one of her trips down here.

He went back to the database that listed all children from the Solomon Clinic. Jackpot. She was on the list. But after a few times, her mother had stopped bringing her back for testing. And Carson's father had never brought him back.

Harold scrolled through her record. Her parents had

been a wealthy couple who had probably thought that rules and contracts didn't apply to them. They had died in a small plane crash on the way to their vacation house. Their main residence was in Frederick, and Olivia had inherited it after their deaths. He found an interior design magazine that featured her work, as well as pictures of her workshop that looked like a converted old carriage house. There were mentions of awards in the local paper and even in the *Baltimore Sun* and *Washington Post*.

He rubbed a hand over the stubble on his chin. Her notoriety presented a problem. Carson had been a nobody fishing-charter captain. She was a local celebrity. If he had her shot after interrogation, the police were going to do some investigating. Better to arrange an accident at sea for both her and Gabe Bowman. Yeah, maybe they'd been dating or something and had gone out cruising—and met with some nautical disaster.

But he was back to square one as far as his assessment of the Solomon Clinic spawn. Travis was dead, and there weren't any other clinic children for her to hook up with. How the hell had she gotten tangled up in the detective's investigation?'

Still, something out of the ordinary had happened to Roka. Did she have some powers on her own? Like he had suspected with Carson? Or was it some trick the detective had been able to pull off? It would have to be a trick, because there was no reason for him to have any para-normal powers.

Harold sat down at the computer, reviewing the videos

that the cameras had taken of the car. Roka hadn't been able to describe what had happened. As he watched, Harold couldn't either. He just knew that something very odd had gone down.

Well, maybe he couldn't get to the bottom of it—yet. But he wasn't going to take any chances. When he scooped up the woman, he was going to make sure she was incapacitated before getting anywhere near her.

OLIVIA WAVERED on her feet and glanced up to see Gabe giving her a critical look. "You need to get some sleep. But we should eat something first. Um, is there anything around we can grab?"

"I'm not much of a cook, but I have takeout from some of the best restaurants and delis in town."

"What do we have?"

"Let's find out." She led him to the kitchen and began taking cartons from the fridge.

Gabe selected some kung pao chicken. Needing something lighter, she went for a beet salad with grapefruit, feta cheese, and pistachio nuts.

"You actually like beets?" he asked, as he waited for the microwave to warm up his food.

"Yes. Try them. You may like them."

"I'll leave them for you."

It was fully dark by the time she and Travis went

upstairs to her bed, where she changed into sweatpants and a T-shirt.

"You're wondering if you're going to have to make a quick getaway," Travis said.

"Unfortunately, I can't lie to you," she answered.

GODDARD RARELY WENT on missions with his operatives, but this time was an exception. There had been too many cock-ups lately, and he was going to make damn sure nothing else untoward happened.

He selected two good men, not including Roka. One of them, Kentwell, had been on the kidnap operation. The other, Green, had not been along, but he was an excellent choice for the evening's work. He had a lot of technical experience, he knew how to work quickly and quietly, and he was a helicopter pilot.

He had Green prep the helo as he looked at some online maps for a suitable landing spot. Not near the Langston house, because that might alert her. Was the detective keeping her company? That would be convenient. They could deal with him at the same time.

After finding a landing place, he arranged for a vehicle to be on site when he got there.

Harold quickly gathered the equipment he needed. It also helped that Olivia Langston's house was an old one. There'd be lots of opportunities for penetration.

Everything was in place before midnight.

He was whistling a jaunty tune as he went out to board the helicopter. Soon he'd know exactly what had happened to Roka.

CHAPTER EIGHTEEN

Travis knew something was wrong. First, there was the muzzy feeling in his head. It shouldn't be there. He had no body, no physical brain that was failing to function. Still, he had to fight for coherent thoughts. The only firm idea that stuck in his mind was that Olivia was in danger.

Fear and something else he couldn't identify would have cut off his airways if he had needed air to breathe. Feeling a deep stab of dread, he turned to Olivia in the darkness. *Wake up. You have to wake up.*

In response, she made a choking sound and started to cough. *Yes. Wake up,* he urged.

She blinked, her eyes drifting partially open, but she didn't come any closer to consciousness.

Something's going on. Desperately, he tried to reach her mind, but his thoughts were too fuzzy to do it. And he sensed that hers were even more impaired.

Summoning every ounce of strength he could pull

together, he grasped her shoulder, but he got no further response from her.

Desperation kept him trying to break through to her. *You have to wake up. You have to get out of here.*

But it was already too late for escape. The bedroom door burst open, and figures rushed in. In his stupor-like state, he couldn't figure out exactly what they were. Animals? Men?

They had recognizable arms, legs, and bodies, but there was something badly wrong with their faces. Instead of noses, they had elongated snouts like something out of a horror movie. Or an old Star Trek episode he'd seen in reruns about a salt monster that sucked the life out of people

Then the shapes came clear to him, and he realized that they were all men, all wearing gas masks. Which must mean they were protecting themselves from something.

The whole picture suddenly came to him in a flash of insight. Before coming in, they must have found a way to flood the house with poison gas.

Poison, oh God, no! He leaned over Olivia, feeling the breath moving in and out of her nose. Whatever it was hadn't killed her—at least not yet. But it had knocked her as senseless as a stone statue. And it had made his thoughts muzzy because he was tied to her.

One of them spoke. "Looks like she's out, too."

Too? That must mean that Gabe was also incapacitated. So the stuff was all over the house. How had they done it?

And Christ, what was he going to do now? He tried again to wake Olivia, but he got no response. Next, he turned to the men and tried to zap them the way he and Olivia had done with the tin cans. But it was no good. He could barely raise a trickle of power. Not on his own and not in his present state, maybe because he and Olivia had drained themselves during their manic practice session. They'd been frantically trying to get ready for trouble. They hadn't realized how close the danger was, and that they were simply making themselves more vulnerable than ever.

If he could have spoken, he would have filled the room with curses.

"How soon before the gas dissipates?"

"I don't know exactly. Don't take any chances. Keep your masks on."

The command sent a shiver up Travis's spine. Not so much the words, but the voice from his nightmares. It was Smith. Against all reason, he was here, at Olivia's house. Somehow, he had found out who she was and where she lived.

Trying desperately to protect her, Travis threw himself across her body, but he had no substance and no damn power. One of the men leaned right through him and rolled her over, grasping her hands so he could cuff her wrists behind her back. Next, he tied her ankles together so that she had no hope of escape. Overkill. But they were taking no chances.

The man straightened, staring down at his captive before looking back at Smith. "That was odd."

"What?"

"When I leaned over her, I felt something."

"What?" the hated voice demanded.

"I don't know. Can't describe it." He lifted a shoulder. "Like there was something in my way. I had to push through it.

"Air currents?"

"I dunno."

"Well, it doesn't matter," came the clipped response. "We're getting out of here while the getting's good."

The other man lifted Olivia over one shoulder like a sack of grain and clasped her bottom as he started for the door.

Travis leaped to block his way, but the energy he and Olivia had generated was simply gone. Still, the guy looked back, probably feeling the same sensation as when he'd leaned down to secure his captive.

Travis clenched his fists, feeling defeat settle over him like one of those heavy blankets they laid over you before they X-rayed your teeth. If he could have thought straight, maybe there was something he could have done. But any realistic course of action eluded him. All he could do was follow along as Smith led the way, and the other guy followed with Olivia.

They reached the den, where they joined up with another man also wearing a gas mask and standing over

Gabe. The detective was also out cold and trussed up like a pork roast.

"Time to leave," Smith muttered, and the two men marched forward with their inert captives.

They came out onto the driveway where an SUV was waiting. When the cargo was loaded inside, the captors all climbed aboard. One of them drove. The other stayed in the back, where the bodies were laid out. Travis squeezed into a bit of remaining space.

Had this car really gotten here so quickly from the Eastern Shore? The mystery of the fast arrival was solved when they came to an open field where a helicopter was waiting.

The SUV pulled to the side, and the cargo was unloaded into the helo. Then they took off with all aboard, including Travis.

On the ride back, Travis scanned the landscape below. He knew the area well and kept his eye out for landmarks as they flew. He recognized Annapolis, then the Bay Bridge. As they approached St. Stephens, he kept his eyes on the roads below. It wasn't that easy to follow the route, but he thought he could see which turns they were taking, and when they came to a large estate, he saw that it backed onto the Miles River. That must be the river Pete had been talking about. The property was vast, with green lawns, several outbuildings, and a house that was probably the manor of a former plantation.

The helo came down by a large barn which had been modified to serve as the hangar.

More men were waiting on the ground for Smith to arrive, and snapped to attention when he started giving orders.

"Get her into the interrogation room," he barked.

"What about the detective?" one of the operatives asked.

Smith glanced at the unconscious man. "Secure him in a cell. I'll decide what to do with him later."

The tone of his voice told Travis it might be a one-way trip. Or maybe the bastard would decide to see what he could get out of Gabe.

Keep him alive. He might have information about Olivia, Travis silently projected toward Smith. Could he influence a person's actions? He didn't know, but what did he have to lose?

FAR AWAY IN the guesthouse on the Bordeaux plantation in Lafayette, Louisiana, Rachel Harper awoke. Her husband was instantly aware that something had jolted her from sleep.

"What?" he asked, alarm making his heart start to pound. "Are we in danger? Under attack?"

"No, not us."

"Then what?"

"The people in Maryland I told you about."

He relaxed a fraction. "The...unusual ones?"

"Yes. The couple where he's dead and she was able to

keep him from crossing over."

When Jake dragged in a breath and let it out in a rush, Rachel knew that he was still reserving judgment on her belief that one of the pair was already deceased.

"She's been drugged and captured by the guy who tried to get Stephanie and Craig. The same guy who killed..." She paused, trying to bring the name into focus. "Who killed Travis."

"That's the ghost? That's his name?"

"Yes." She sat up and ran a hand through his hair.

"And you know all this, how...?"

"Travis is beyond desperate. He's trying to get through to...Olivia, but he can't do it because Smith put her under."

"Smith?" Jake had also pushed himself up and was looking questioningly at his wife.

"I'm only getting this because Travis is so agitated. He's putting out the strongest signal I've ever felt."

Jake whistled through his teeth. "And he's a ghost?"

Rachel went on with her explanation of the situation. "Obviously, Smith is a false name. But I'm willing to bet he's the one who went after Stephanie and Craig—and then Elizabeth and Matt."

They were the most recent couple who had joined the group of telepaths who had established a base of operation at Gabriella Bordeaux's plantation. Gabriella ran a restaurant in the manor house where she and Luke lived. The others were in the guesthouses Gabriella's mom had rented out before her death. And the group was having several more cottages constructed in case other children from the Solomon clinic showed up.

"Bet your life?" Jake shot back.

Rachel went on as though her husband hadn't spoken. "Smith tortured Travis before he killed him. Olivia and a detective were trying to find out Smith's real identity. But he found them first. It looks like he made sure the pair were unconscious before he scooped them up."

"Her and the detective, you mean?"

"Yes. Smith doesn't know Travis is along for the ride. Apparently, he has to stay near Olivia." She paused for a moment, assessing the situation. "They've, uh, bonded in a way that I can't describe. It's really quite extraordinary."

Jake swore under his breath. "And I suppose you want to go charging off to help them."

"Yes," she answered in a firm voice.

"And why do you think they won't attack us?"

"They're in no position to attack. They're in trouble." She glared at Jake in the dim light coming in through the window.

"Have any of the couples we rescued been anything but grateful? And don't throw Mickey and Kira in my face. I think we both know Kira was a psychopath, and Mickey would have done anything she asked of him."

She saw Jake clench his fists. "Where are—is it Olivia and Travis?"

"Yes. They're on the Eastern Shore of Maryland."

"If we leave now, it's going to take hours for us to get there. And it might be too late by the time we do."

"But we have to try. And probably the best couple to take with us are Elizabeth and Matt, if they're willing. Matt learned his survival skills in Africa. And they both know the area."

"Baltimore isn't exactly the Eastern Shore."

Rachel was already out of bed and picking up her cell phone. "We need to tell the others and see what they think."

CHAPTER NINETEEN

Travis tried to raise some kind of power to stop what was happening. But he was too deadened to have any effect. The drug Smith had given Olivia had done its work.

With a leaden feeling of defeat, he watched while she was secured to a stretcher, then followed along as the men wheeled her into the house like a patient from an ambulance being rushed into the hospital. Only this was no hospital. He had been here before, and he knew it was a torture chamber—with only one exit.

He shuddered, then forced himself to take in details he'd had no chance to see before. Because he'd been covered like a special delivery package the last time he was here, he hadn't seen the outside of the house or any of the interior besides that room where he'd spent his last hours as a living man. Now, if he had had blood in his veins, it would have frozen as he watched them bring her to the same place. He couldn't stop himself from shaking. And it took everything he had to prevent himself from turning around and fleeing. But he stayed because there was no way he was going to just leave Olivia to Smith's tender mercies.

She was the only thing that kept him here. He hovered close to her as the men transferred her to the same table where Smith had tortured him. Horror clutched his chest as he watched them secure her arms and legs.

God, no. Don't let him hurt her, he prayed over and over before switching his focus to the man who had complete control over her now.

You don't want to hurt her. There's no reason to hurt her. She can't give you any helpful information, he projected.

He tried to grab Smith's arm as the torture master leaned possessively over his new specimen like a butterfly collector inspecting a recent acquisition.

At Travis's touch, the man flinched and looked quickly over his shoulder, right into Travis's enraged gaze.

"What?" he mouthed.

Do you see me?

Smith only stared, then shook his head. "There's nobody here but me and the woman," he said aloud.

Wrong, Travis answered, but the monster didn't hear him. He'd need more power to get through to Smith, and right now there was no source of power. Not from Olivia and not from himself. How long would it take to get it back? He didn't know. He didn't know if Smith would drug her again. He didn't know any damn thing except that he had to somehow save her. It couldn't all end like this, in this house with this man. Not after what he and Olivia had created together.

After a charged moment, the kidnapper shrugged and went back to his captive.

He raised first one and then the other of Olivia's eyelids and inspected her pupils. They were dark and dilated, and Travis watched Smith stroke his chin with thumb and forefinger as he leaned over her.

"How safe is it to bring you to consciousness?" he whispered.

Very safe, Travis answered. *Go ahead and wake her up; that's the most efficient way to question her. You want her to be coherent.*

And I want to be able to connect with her again, he silently added.

But the bastard didn't seem to pay any attention to him. Or maybe Travis had had some effect, and he couldn't tell.

"I need to have you partly conscious," Smith said. "Let's wait a little while for you to start coming around. I'll be right outside, but I'll be watching for any signs of life." He chuckled. "Not like your friend Carson. He's beyond that."

You'd be surprised, Travis silently answered.

Had Smith decided on his own to wait to question Olivia, or had Travis influenced him? He wished he knew.

OLIVIA WAS DREAMING. She was snuggled in bed with Travis, and he wasn't a ghost. He was alive. They were like any normal couple. Only they had more than anyone else. They had a special bond that gave them powers.

That's what she wanted to be true, but in the back of her mind she knew she was lying to herself. Something was wrong—badly wrong. And the only way she could find out what was to wake up.

She didn't want to. The dream was better. But she heard a voice calling her, telling her she had to be prepared.

Following it, she struggled toward consciousness. Where was she? Not in her bed with Travis. The surface under her body felt hard. Not a bed. But where?

Somewhere far in the distance she thought she heard Travis calling her. Or did she? It was hard to be sure. Why couldn't she reach out to him the way she was used to doing?

Still, she thought he was speaking in her head. *Don't move. That will give you a little more time, let him think you're totally unconscious.* She heard his words, but not with the clarity she expected. It was as though he was close by but at the same far away.

Desperately she struggled to knit the connection together.

Travis?

Whatever you do, don't say my name. Don't let him know that you ever met me.

Why?

Smith has you.

Fear leaped inside her. Smith...had...how?

Travis was speaking urgently, and now his words were a little clearer although they didn't make total sense.

He's dangerous. God knows what he'll do if he knows you have anything to do with me. Don't let him catch on. You have to play dumb.

She struggled with confusion. *But I do know you.*

You can't let him find out.

She was about to answer when the door slammed open, and a man came charging into the room. He was holding something in his hand, but she couldn't see what it was.

"Are you awake?" he demanded.

She licked her dry lips. "A little."

"Good. That's good."

"I...I need a drink," she said. It was true, but she was also stalling for time. Her thoughts were too muddled for her to figure out what she should do.

"Maybe after you answer some questions," he said.

"Who are you?" she asked, when she knew the answer perfectly well. There was only one person he could be. And Travis had told her who he was. He was the monster who had killed Travis. And now he had her.

"I want to ask you some questions. How do you know Travis Carson?"

Deep confusion swirled in her brain. Hadn't Travis spoken to her a little while ago? Hadn't he told her not to say she knew him? It was on the tip of her tongue to answer yes, when Travis's hand came down over her lips. *Be quiet about me. Don't tell him anything,* he implored. The urgency in his voice told her he was terrified—for her.

Still confused, she tried to move her arm and found that it was secured by a strap to the table she was lying on. Not just that arm. The other one, too. And her legs. When she realized she was strapped down, panic rose in her throat.

Where was she? What had happened? The last thing she remembered was going to sleep last night. And now she was somewhere else.

As she was trying to process that, she felt another touch. Not Travis's gentle fingers.

Suddenly, the situation and Travis's urgent instructions became clear. Smith had taken her. She had been sure he couldn't find her, but somehow he had, and he was holding her captive, the way he had held Travis. And she knew Travis had had only a short time to live after he left this room.

Seconds after that horrible moment of realization, Smith's hand came down hard against her cheek, making her skin sting, and her eyes water. They blinked open, focusing on her captor. He didn't look imposing. He was old, with thinning, salt-and-pepper hair, and veins that stood out. One in his neck was throbbing now. Maybe he'd have a stroke, and this would all be over.

"How do you know Travis Carson," he growled.

She blinked again, trying to focus, and saw the hand moving again, getting ready for another strike if she stayed silent. "I don't," she cried out. "Who?"

"Travis Carson. Don't lie to me. If you don't know Carson, why were you with Bowman?"

Why indeed?

Travis had told her not to admit anything. But how could she pull that off? Somehow, this man had seen her with Gabe. That was an immutable fact. Why had she been with Gabe? He'd told her to stay hidden. She had thought she knew better. Answers sprang to her lips, none of them any good. Her mind was too muzzy for her to think straight. But she knew that she couldn't put it on Gabe— Lord knows what Smith would do to him if he thought Gabe had come looking for her.

And she was the only one who could stop Smith from realizing that Travis was still here. What would happen if he knew *that?*

She scrambled for an answer that would make sense and satisfy this horrible man. *I have to tell him something* she finally said to Travis, and she felt him follow her logic and come to the same conclusion.

"I knew him...a long time ago," she finally said.

"Where?"

"At the clinic."

"What clinic?" the monster pressed.

"Dr. Solomon's clinic. I used to go there with the other children."

Smith kept his gaze locked on her, and she wondered if he believed her answer. "Why were you there?" he demanded.

She raised a shoulder. "I think they were testing us."

"For what?"

"I was just a little kid. I don't know."

Smith was looking thoughtful. "But that doesn't explain how the two of you got together recently."

This time, Travis supplied the answer. *I recognized you. I asked to have coffee with you so we could talk. I'm dead. He can't prove otherwise.*

Hysteria threatened to bubble up in her throat, but she held it in check. "One day when I was in town delivering furniture, he saw me. He said we had met before."

Smith's eyes lit up, then dulled. Probably he was excited to prove his theory that she was connected to Travis but kicking himself that he had already killed the man, so he couldn't find out what they could do together.

That thought brought a spurt of hope. What could they do?

She reached for Travis in the way they had developed, but it was no good. Her brain was still fogged, and she could barely talk to him, let alone do anything more.

What are we going to do? she asked in desperation.

His answer was no comfort. *I don't know.*

She knew Smith couldn't see Travis, but she could. His

face was suffused with horror and regret, as the man who had killed him hovered over her.

He turned away from her and went to his laptop, where he called up a list of names, scrolling rapidly through the entries. She watched him anxiously, wondering what was coming next. Closing her eyes, she turned her head away. The next thing she knew, he was shaking her—hard.

His voice was a low, menacing growl as he said, "The Howell Institute doesn't have Carson as one of the children who were brought back to the clinic for testing."

She feigned surprise. "Huh?"

Smith shook her again. "The Howell Institute. He's not listed as a returnee."

She stared up at the man, trying to order her thoughts.

Stick to your story, Travis told her.

"I don't know what you're talking about. Are you saying I didn't meet Travis at the clinic? That's wrong."

Anger flared on Smith's face. "It says he didn't go back."

"I...can't help that," she answered, trying to put some substance behind the words.

"And how did Bowman find you?"

Travis moved to her side. *Tell him he said he saw your name on a list of children from the clinic.*

"Uh, he said he saw my name on a list of children from the clinic."

"That list is very private."

"Well, it's what he said."

Travis's voice was urgent. *We have to make sure Gabe gives him the same story. He saw your name on the Howell Institute list.*

But how can you speak to him mind-to-mind?

I don't know. But I have to do it. He went on rapidly. *Keep Smith here while I try to reach Gabe. And, if you can, send me power.*

I don't think I can.

Try. Keep trying.

Before she could respond, she knew Travis had left the room.

Olivia clenched her fists. Keep this monster here? That was the last thing she wanted to do, but she knew that Travis was right. She and Gabe had to have the same story.

"Who are you?" she asked in a weak voice. "Why did you bring me here? Where are we, anyway?"

He turned back to her. "You can call me Mr. Smith."

It was a relief to hear the name. Now she didn't have to pretend she didn't know who he was.

"And why did you bring me here?"

"Because you showed up outside Travis Carson's house when the detective dragged my man in there."

She shuddered.

"Why were you there, exactly?" he demanded.

"I wanted to—help out."

"Why?"

"Travis had approached me in town. I liked him."

Smith's gaze turned speculative. "And what kind of reaction did you have to him?"

How much should she say? What would Smith believe? He knew a lot about the clinic and the children. "I was attracted to him."

"Did you do anything about it?"

"I...didn't want to get involved."

Smith leaned over her, his eyes sharp. "But you felt a pull toward him."

She opened her mouth and closed it again.

"Did you fuck him?"

Oh Lord, what should she say?

His fingers closed painfully over her arm, and he shook her roughly.

"Did you fuck him?" he asked again.

"No."

"Why not? Weren't you attracted to him?"

"Yes." She focused on the pain of his fingers on her arm. It was helping her brain function again. "But there was an intensity between us. It gave me a headache."

"Ah." Smith looked excited now.

"That scared me. I'd never felt anything like that before. I ran away from him. Maybe that was why I felt so bad when that detective said he was dead."

Smith gave her another good shake and pushed away from her. "Well, that's a new one," he muttered. "Are you lying?"

"Why would I lie?"

He shook his head. "Maybe I'd better find out what the detective knows about it." He considered for a moment. "And how did you hook up with the detective anyway?"

"He approached me."

"Why?"

"I'm not sure. He said something about a list."

"So you say."

Smith turned toward the door, and Olivia felt a spurt of relief—followed immediately by panic. Had Travis been able to contact Gabe?

She remembered then that he had asked her to send him power. Was there any hope she could do it?

With everything she could summon, she reached for Travis and could just barely feel him at the edge of her awareness. Was he too far away for her to send him anything? And did she have any energy to send?

AFTER ONE LAST look at Olivia, Travis turned away and slipped through the wall into a hallway. As he got farther away, he could feel the link with Olivia stretching. How far could he get from her? And what would happen if he got too far? His pace slowed, but he realized that would do him no good. If he couldn't get to Gabe, they were in deep shit.

When he felt like he could hardly move another inch farther from her, he finally reached the room where Gabe was stashed. That was a good sign, he told himself. At least he had enough awareness of the man to find him.

Stepping through the wall, he found himself in a small,

dark chamber set up like a cell. Gabe was lying on a hard bunk, his hands and legs bound and his eyes closed.

Okay. Now he was here. But that was only a small part of what he had to accomplish. He had to get through to the man and tell him the story that would save Olivia. Was there any way to do that?

He looked around and spotted a camera up at ceiling level. The prisoner was being watched. That was an unfortunate complication.

Although he'd never talked directly to the other man, he had to do it now. But how? They'd been together for a while—maybe he could reach him. He had to because Olivia's life or her freedom might depend on it. There was no telling what torture Smith would put her through if he knew she had her own private ghost.

He flexed his fingers, then reached to put a hand on the detective's shoulder. At first, there was no response. Using what power he could summon, he shook the man. It wasn't much. Nothing like the effort he'd put out when he'd rocked Pete's car. But it was *something*. More of his energy must be coming back. And maybe somehow Olivia was helping him.

Gabe's eyes flew open. "Waaa?" He looked around, seeing no one.

It's Travis. You have to focus on what I'm saying. You have to listen.

The plea got no response. Instead, Gabe began testing his bonds. Handcuffs secured his wrists, but his legs were tied with rope. Pulling his legs toward his hands, he began to work at the bonds.

Travis put his hand over the knot Gabe was working on, and he went still, glancing around. He started to speak but then thought better of it. Good man. He must have figured out that anything he said could be overheard. Still, he seemed perplexed as his features took on a strained look, like he was trying to remember a name he couldn't quite recall. *Is that you, Travis?*

Yes! Thank God you can hear me.

Gabe shook his head. *If it's you, give me a sign.*

Travis pressed his hand against Gabe's.

Okay, I felt that. Or is it a hallucination?

It's me.

Maybe I heard something. I'm not sure.

Travis wanted to shout in frustration but calmed himself. He wasn't exactly getting through, but there had to be a way to do it.

He moved his finger against the back of Gabe's hand and wrote. "In S's house. U never heard of him."

Gabe gave a fraction of a nod.

Travis wrote, "Wants to know why O was with U."

The next part was harder, but he laboriously spelled out the crux of the message. "U read Howell Institute records."

Howell Institute?

"Y"

Again, he laboriously spelled out, "O said she met me there as a kid. And you saw her name on the list."

Gabe shook his head. *Not sure I'm getting this.*

Travis tried to write fast. "Big danger if S knows O comms with me now."

Gabe sagged against the bunk. *I don't know...*

"Remember her name on the Howell Institute list. U don't know S."

Before Travis could write more, the door slammed open, and a man barreled into the room, a look of fury on his face. Who else could it be but Smith?

CHAPTER TWENTY

Gabe tipped his head to the side, staring at the man who must have gone to a lot of trouble to capture him and Olivia.

Smith charged across the floor. "What happened a few minutes ago?"

So he'd been right—he was under observation. Now he did his best to look confused. "I dunno. A nightmare?" He tried to lift an arm. "Um, who are you? Why am I trussed up like a Christmas goose?"

"I'm asking the questions."

"Tell me who you are," Gabe pressed.

"As far as you're concerned, I'm Mr. Smith. And I want some answers from you—now."

Well, that was fortunate, since Gabe had been worried about saying the name by accident.

"What if I don't want to give them?" he asked.

Smith answered by drawing back a fist and socking

him in the face. It felt like a bone might have crunched. He wasn't sure.

"This is what happens."

"I'm not telling you anything."

Another blow, another blast of pain. Smith leaned over and hauled him up by the shirt collar. "I want to know how you found out Langston was connected to Carson."

So Travis had been right. Smith must want to know why Olivia had shown up when he dragged Pete into Travis's house. Yeah, right, why would she, if she didn't know Travis? "Detective work," Gabe spat out. The words were accompanied by flecks of blood. But not any teeth.

"I don't want your smart answers. I want the real ones. How did Langston and Carson know each other? How did *you* know her?"

Was Travis still here, watching? Gabe looked around and thought maybe he saw a vague shape just beyond Smith.

He was going to have to answer, and in fact it had better be the right answer. Travis wanted him to convince Smith that this wasn't a ghost story—that Travis and Olivia had gotten together while he was still alive. He licked his bruised lip.

"You want to know how I found the connection?"

"Yes, dammit."

"Uh," He struggled to get it right. "The Howell Institute."

"And how the hell would you know anything about it?"

Now what? Or what the hell? Smith probably knew about Decorah Security.

"My agency," he said, "we have access to all kinds of information."

"That's classified Top Secret. More than Top Secret. How the hell would you get access to the list?"

"Top Secret," Gabe replied. "For some people, maybe."

That earned him another blow to the face. At this rate, he was going to look like he'd gone ten rounds with Mike Tyson.

He spoke carefully through his bruised lips. "People hire us because we have resources others don't."

"But Carson's name wasn't on the list of children who were brought back for testing."

Gabe thought fast. "But his mother was on the other list, right? The list of women who were treated there."

Smith swore as he stared down at Gabe. "You'd better not be lying." The man's eyes narrowed. "How did *you* get together with her?"

"Her mother was on the list," he said.

"If you're lying, you'll be sorry," Smith answered.

I'm already sorry, Gabe thought. Aloud, he said, "What would be the point of lying?"

"Misdirection," his captor snarled.

Gabe said nothing. This guy was already wound up tighter than the mainspring of a mousetrap.

As Smith exited the room, Gabe breathed a little prayer, then reached for Travis. But the ghost was gone, probably back with Olivia.

When Travis had first come to his cell, Gabe hadn't understood the urgency of the discussion he was going to have with Smith. Now he thought he did. If the killer knew that Travis was still around, no telling what he'd do to Olivia to find out exactly what was going on.

He hadn't given that away. One problem solved, but he had another one. Maybe now that he'd given up what Smith considered vital information, Gabe Bowman was expendable.

Too bad. Probably he was heading rapidly toward the end of his career, because he couldn't think of a way this was going to end happily for either him or Olivia.

Thinking of her sent a pang through him. She probably didn't know he was attracted to her. To her strength. To her artistic ability. To her Renaissance beauty, although her other qualities would have drawn him without that amazing exterior. If she hadn't already been bonded to Travis, Gabe would have tried to get something going with her. Not that it would have done him any good. According to her, the children born as a result of the treatments at the Solomon Clinic could only have fulfilling relationships with each other. And he wasn't one of them. Daydreaming about getting in bed with her wasn't going to do him any good. It would be more productive to figure out how to get out of this mess.

Or maybe there was no way out. He made his hands as small as possible, trying to slip them through the loops of the handcuffs. It was wasted effort.

HAROLD GODDARD, alias Mr. Smith, stood in the hallway, clenching and unclenching his fists. He'd gotten himself into a cluster fuck. Capturing and sending Carson to the afterlife had been no problem. Nobody was going to miss him—well, except unfortunately, the aunt Harold hadn't known about. Too bad she'd called up a detective agency that could somehow tap into classified information. Should he dispose of her, too?

He answered his own question with a tight shake of his head. Too many bodies piling up were going to be noticed. And cops might start tying the cases together, although they probably didn't have the Howell Institute's lists. And wouldn't know what they meant if they stumbled on them.

But Harold was still about as exposed as a roach lying in a bag of rice. He was going to have to give up this very nice estate and get the hell out of St. Stephens. At the end of his quasi-government career, he'd vanished into thin air. He could do it again and start over with another identity. That left a major question. Should he keep probing the powers of the children from the Solomon Clinic? If he did, he was going to have to be a lot more careful. But one thing he knew for certain—he had to get rid of both Gabe Bowman and Olivia Langston in a way no one could tie to him or this estate.

Right now, both of them were a problem. It looked like Bowman worked for a very effective security agency.

They'd want to know what happened to their operative. And Olivia was a well-known local artist who had gained a national reputation. If her body were found somewhere with a bullet in its head, the cops were going to start digging for answers. Both she and Gabe Bowman would have to die in an accident. Together would be best. Maybe when they'd started working together, they'd gotten involved and decided to take off somewhere romantic together.

What if they burned up in a car crash? On the face of it, that sounded like a good solution. But another idea was seeping into his mind, gaining a firmer place in his imagination. The notion was being put there by the invisible man standing behind him, projecting vivid pictures into his head.

SOMEHOW, Travis had developed a new talent. Somehow, he was able to sense Smith's thoughts and maybe influence them.

Knowing what the man was thinking was almost unbearable. It brought a sick feeling bubbling up inside him. If he'd had a body, he was sure stomach acid would be rising in a burning tide up his throat.

Smith was still in the hall, looking a lot less confident than he'd been a few hours earlier. Good.

Before he could open the door of the torture chamber, Travis walked through the wall.

Olivia's eyes instantly sought his.

What happened? Were you able to communicate with Gabe?

Travis described the method he'd used.

Clever.

It was a desperate move.

And she knew he was still feeling desperate.

What aren't you telling me? It's something bad, right?

The last part wasn't a question, but a statement of fact. When she pulled the information from his mind, she made a small choking sound. Although she'd been pretty sure of Smith's ultimate plans for her and Gabe, confirmation was like suddenly having her breath choked off.

He's planning to kill us. He thinks that will put an end to his problems.

Travis wanted to tell her everything was going to be okay, but he couldn't choke out the words. All he could promise was:

We have a big advantage.

What?

He doesn't know I'm here.

But we're weak.

Yeah. He paused for a moment before continuing. *I, uh, sense something.*

Like what?

Someone is trying to contact me.

What do you mean?

Someone is trying to talk to me. I mean in my head, like we're talking.

Who?

Do you remember when Smith first captured me, and he kept telling me about other couples who were children from the clinic?

Yes.

It's one of them, I think.

Why can you hear them and I can't?

He shook his head. *Maybe because I'm dead and you're not?*

Yeah.

She might have said more, but Smith strode into the room. "Good news," he said. "I'm going to let you go."

For a moment, hope rose in her chest, until she realized it had to be a lie. She knew too much.

Glancing at Travis, she saw the devastated look on his face. She wanted to whisper, "It's not your fault." But no way could she give away to Smith that he was in the room with them.

CHAPTER TWENTY-ONE

"Do you know how to find the estate?" Stephanie Branson asked Rachel.

"I think so."

The six members of the team from Louisiana had landed at BWI International Airport and rented a van. As a group, they had decided that Rachel and Jake Harper should go on the rescue mission, along with Matt Delano, Elizabeth Forester, and Stephanie and Craig Branson. Gabriella Bordeaux and Luke Buckley had stayed home because she had to keep the restaurant open to make it look like everything was normal at the Bordeaux plantation.

The team had already crossed the Bay Bridge and were speeding down Route 50, heading for St. Stephens, when Rachel gasped.

"What's wrong?" Jake demanded.

"Smith is getting ready to kill Olivia and Gabe Bowman, the detective who was investigating Travis's death." She had already filled the group in on the players, so they understood the situation.

"Smith," Stephanie muttered.

"And we still don't have his real name?"

"Unfortunately, no."

Still, they were pretty sure he was the same guy who had tried to kidnap Stephanie and later Matt and Elizabeth.

On the way from New Orleans to Baltimore, Rachel had told them as much as she knew. They understood that Gabe wasn't one of the children from the Solomon Clinic. He'd gotten caught in Smith's net when he was investigating Travis's death.

Rachel had been getting ready to direct Jake to Smith's estate, but suddenly she gasped.

"What is it?" Stephanie asked.

"Smith's going to deep-six Olivia and Gabe. Change of plans. Instead of heading for his estate, we have to get to the town dock and rent a boat."

Rachel turned to Jake. "Can you drive any faster?"

"If we get stopped by a cop, that will only slow us down," he answered.

OLIVIA HAD BECOME an expert at reading Smith's expressions. He was trying to look reassuring, but he couldn't hide the malevolence just below the surface.

"We're going for a boat ride," he said. "I'll leave you

and the detective off on an uninhabited island. That way, you'll have a fighting chance."

Oh sure, she thought. He was trying to make this like one of those survival reality TV shows. But since any comment she made would only make things worse, she kept silent.

His eyes narrowed. "You look like you're plotting something."

"No."

Ignoring her protest, he went on, "That would be a mistake. Don't spoil anything by trying to get away. I wouldn't want to have to shoot you. My men are bringing Carson's boat to my dock. After they let you off, they'll come back and leave the boat drifting. It will look like there was an emergency on board and you had to abandon ship."

Travis had moved beside her and stood with his hand protectively on her shoulder. She saw Smith squint, and a spurt of alarm crossed his face. "What's that?" he demanded.

"What's what?"

"I thought I saw..." His voice trailed off.

She might have asked what he had seen, but she suspected that would only earn her a hard slap across the face. And when she sensed Travis getting ready to fly at the man, she shouted a warning in her head. *No. That will only make him start questioning me about you.*

Regret and anger flashed in Travis's eyes, and she saw him clench his fists. *Unfortunately, that's right.*

Hopefully we'll get a chance to smack his self-satisfied

face, she answered, praying it was true. It would be a miracle if they got out of this alive.

Travis's inner voice was gritty. *I wish we were strong enough to kill him now. But we're not. And if we try, we'll make him change his plans. He'll move up his timetable and kill you now.*

She winced at the blunt words, but she knew they had to be realistic.

We need to make some plans of our own.

During the silent conversation, Smith had turned away, and she couldn't see what he was doing. Suddenly, he whirled toward her, and she saw with alarm that he had a hypodermic in his hand. Instinctively she tried to pull away, but the table held her fast. And before she could take two breaths, he jabbed the needle into her arm.

"No," she cried out in anguish.

"I'm not taking any chances with your being able to do something tricky. I'll be back for you when we're ready to leave.

She desperately clawed at consciousness, but she felt it slipping away. In her mind, she could hear Travis cursing. *We should have taken a chance. We should have tried to blast him.*

That was the last thing she heard.

THE GROUP from Louisiana headed straight for the St.

Stephens town dock, and paid a premium to rent a fast boat.

As soon as they cleared the marina, they headed down-river toward the Chesapeake Bay. They had no fixed destination. All they could do was make for the location of the...ghost who was now guiding Rachel toward open water. It felt weird to call him that, but she couldn't think of another word to describe him.

Because of their speed, the telepaths were able to catch up while the other vessel was still heading out to sea. As the rescue party drew near, they used their combined efforts to make their craft disappear from view so that the thugs had no idea that they were being followed.

At the same time, Rachel's contact with...the ghost grew stronger.

Call me Travis, he told her. That's my name. Thank you for showing up. I was afraid there was no way you could get here in time. I assume you're also part of Dr. Solomon's experiment.

Yes. What's happening, exactly? Rachel asked.

You know about Mr. Smith?

The man who's been trying to capture one of us?

Right. He's given up on trying to find out what we can do. I think he believes it's too dangerous. Which is why men are taking Olivia and Gabe Bowman out to sea now.

And Olivia bonded with you?

Yes.

Which means both you and Olivia are children from the Solomon Clinic.

Yes.

Let me tell the others.

After conveying the information, Rachel said to Travis, *You must have extraordinary powers to have bonded with her...after death.*

No, he corrected her. *I couldn't have done it without Olivia.*

GENTLE ROCKING WOKE OLIVIA. The motion of a boat on the water, she realized. Smith had said he was putting her and Gabe on a boat, and she could smell the tang of the bay. They must be way beyond the river by now. But she could see nothing except what looked like a closed, dark room. She must be somewhere below.

Olivia. Travis's inner voice was urgently saying her name. He had probably been calling to her for a while, trying to wake her up, but she had been beyond his reach. Now that she was coming around, his words penetrated the fog in her brain.

A rough hand shook her, and her eyelids fluttered. They felt like they had been glued together, and it was a tremendous effort to raise them.

"She's waking up."

"Ahead of schedule. The boss said not to let that happen—that she could be dangerous."

"How?"

"Don't know, but we'd better work fast."

She saw one of the men looking over his shoulder.

"What?" the other guy demanded.

"I keep feeling like there's another boat coming up on us fast."

The second guy paused for a moment. "I don't see nothin'."

"But the water. What's making those little waves?"

"Currents," his partner snapped.

As they talked, they were doing something to her ankles. First, they cut off the ropes that bound them, and she had a moment to enjoy the freedom from restraints. Her ankles were raw from the rope, and she wanted to rub some lotion on them. But they weren't going to give her the chance. All too soon, the rope was replaced with something that chafed her skin—something heavy.

Wha?

Weights like in a gym. Christ, they're putting weights on you.

Her brain felt like it was full of cotton candy. Desperate for clarity, she fought for full consciousness, fought to make sense of what was happening.

They lifted her hands, and she felt the cuffs being pulled away. Her wrists felt as raw as her ankles.

"Hurry."

"If the cops find the bodies, won't they think the weights are a little strange?"

"Smith said the outer shell will dissolve after a few hours in water, and the heavy part will sink away."

Somebody lifted her up and slung her over his

shoulder like a side of beef. Then he began to climb a short flight of stairs, wavering as he balanced her weight. In a few moments, she was on deck. She caught a glimpse of Gabe, who looked to be in similar condition.

An island. They were supposed to be heading for an island. She caught no sight of land and remembered that it had been Smith's lie.

But there was something else. It looked like a ghost boat, not quite solid but somehow visible.

She had no time to puzzle that out. No time to say anything to Gabe. In the next moment, she was lofted into the air before crashing down into the water hard enough to sting. The moment she hit, she began to sink. She was a good swimmer, but she simply couldn't keep her head above the surface.

Oh Lord. Suddenly, she flashed back to a terrible memory, the nightmare that had seized her by the throat before she had met Travis. The horrible scene when Smith's men had flung him overboard into the sea. Back then, she had told herself it was only a bad dream, but she had felt it with him. Now it was all happening again. Only this time, she was the one drowning, sinking into the water with no hope of escape.

Desperately, she tried to tread water, but her legs felt like lead. Then she realized the problem. The weights wrapped around her ankles were pulling her down.

RACHEL CAUGHT HER BREATH. *I see Olivia and Gabe now. The men hauled them up on deck. Oh God, they threw her over—then him.*

At that moment, she saw Travis, a vague man shape that certainly wasn't visible to the thugs who had just pitched their victims into the bay. Travis ran to the side of the boat and executed a perfect dive into the water.

As Rachel watched, she keyed into the frantic exchange between her husband, Jake Harper, and Craig Branson:

They're sinking.

And the boat is speeding away.

You go after Olivia, and I'll try to get Gabe, Jake said.

Another water rescue.

It's a lot deeper out here than any bayou.

OLIVIA FLAILED and kicked in despair, trying to force herself upward through the murky water. Somewhere above her, she thought there was sunlight and air. But it might as well have been on the far side of the moon. In her condition, there was no way she could fight the drag of the ankle weights.

Travis was with her, talking to her, ordering her to hold on, saying that help was coming. But it was no good. She was too far down in the watery depths. Cold and darkness closed in around her. Regret tore at her. She remembered people saying that your life flashed before your eyes when you were dying. Something like that happened to her, not all the details, but the sadness of being alone. And then the miracle of Travis finding her. She had basked in the feeling of connection. Oh Lord, if she'd only met him earlier. If they'd only had more time together. But fate had kept them apart for too long and then snatched them away again. Could they find each other in the afterlife? Or was her death the end of everything for them?

She longed to fight for her life, but there was no exit from this final act of her existence. She tried to hold her breath, but then suddenly everything changed. Somehow, there was no more drag on her legs, and a man was lifting her to the surface. She kept trying to hold her breath, but it was no good. Because her lungs were desperate for air, she inhaled—only to drag in seawater.

The choking pain hit her as someone lifted her to the surface, where more hands reached out and grasped her. That was the last she remembered until she began to gasp and choke.

"She's coming around," somebody shouted.

"Thank God. What about the other one?"

The answer came in somber tones. "I've done everything I could, but I'm afraid we've lost him."

Who was speaking? Where was she? On a boat? The same one?

Other people clustered around, but they were all in the background as Travis hovered over her. Even when she'd been unconscious, she'd never lost the connection with him.

A man was talking. Somehow, she knew he was a doctor. "It's too late. He was down too long."

Travis spoke frantically in her mind. *I think I can save him.*

Do it.

He won't be the same. I won't be the same.

She wasn't exactly sure what he meant. Not the same? What? But her conviction was strong. She was alive. Gabe Bowman had tried to help her. It wasn't fair for her to live and for Gabe to die.

Do it, she urged Travis. *If you can save him, do it.*

CHAPTER TWENTY-TWO

Gabe heard voices. Men and women were talking excitedly.

"It's a miracle."

"He was dead." That last was from the one who'd been working on him, trying frantically to bring him back to life. Somehow, he remembered that. He also knew that the man was a doctor.

Gabe tried to breathe, but a coughing fit overtook him.

"Easy. You've had a pretty rough time."

He knew that much. But he struggled to figure out what exactly had happened. Memories seeped into his mind. He'd been tied down in a cell back at Smith's house. His captor had come in with a hypodermic and jabbed him in the arm. Then everything went black until he woke up to feel the rocking of a boat. They were out on the water, and the wind in his face helped revive him. He saw Olivia a few yards away. She looked as dazed as he felt. Then the men were doing something to him, lacing something heavy and clunky around his ankles. Before he could figure out what was going on, he was hoisted up and over the side. He hit the water with a tremendous splash and started to sink.

He'd tried to fight to the surface, but it was no good. He kept sinking, and the terrible need to breathe made him gasp for air and drag in water. Then everything was black again.

His last thoughts had been of failure. He had found Travis's killer, but nobody else would ever know it. Worst of all, he had failed Olivia. He realized now that he should have left her out of his investigation. But he'd dragged her along, and Smith's men had thrown her over the side, too. She didn't deserve to die. Or maybe Travis could save her. He'd clung to that hope as consciousness fled.

And then all at once, he was awake again, feeling the heat of the sun on his face and the motion of a boat on water.

He saw men and women gathered around him. The first word he spoke was, "Olivia."

He heard her gasp his name. "Gabe? You're alive!"

And then a jumble of thoughts and sensations rushed in. His own thoughts, and also not his. The confusion would have been enough to drive him mad—if he'd let it overpower him.

Steady. Everything's going to be okay. Was that Olivia speaking inside his head, the way she'd done with Travis? How was that possible?

What? What the hell is happening? He raised his hand

to his head, pressing against his temple, fighting a headache that threatened to drag him down as surely as the sea had done.

What happened to me? What's happening now?"

A silent voice answered. Not Olivia. Someone else. *I pulled you back. I'm sorry, but it was the only way to save you.*

Sorry? Why should you be sorry?

I'm here with you. It was the only way I could do it.

Travis?

Yes.

Where are you? How can you talk to me like this?

Because I'm in you. I'm part of you. Or you're part of me. I don't know how to say it any better. At least not yet.

Gabe tried to wrap his head around that. *What are you saying?*

You...died. They pulled you up, but Matt couldn't revive you.

Who is Matt?

Matt Delano. He's a doctor. He's one of the children from the Solomon Clinic.

A jolt of panic sizzled through Gabe. He had to be going mad. This couldn't be happening. Whatever *this* was.

He felt a hand clasp his and looked up to see Olivia leaning over him.

"You made it," she murmured. "Other victims of the Solomon Clinic rescued us. We're on their boat, going back to St. Stephens."

At the mention of the town, panic flared. "Smith will find us."

"No. He thinks we're at the bottom of the bay. And we're going to take care of him."

Before he could focus on that, Travis spoke to him, mind to mind in that new weird way.

Do you understand what's happened?

Did he?

You were dead.

Someone had said that before. *I was dead?* He tried to wrap his head around that and failed.

If I was dead, how am I here?

My spirit...infused you—brought you back to life. I'm with you. In your body. In your mind.

Maybe it was finally sinking in. He could either accept the reality of what had happened or he could go mad. He chose sanity.

Thank God. The exclamation came from both Olivia and Travis, and somehow, that was what he needed to ground himself.

He tried to sit up, but the one who was a doctor—Matt Delano—put a hand on his shoulder. "Just lie here for a while. You've been through a pretty nasty ordeal."

"That's putting it mildly," he muttered.

Someone had slipped a pillow under his head and covered him with a blanket. He closed his eyes, drifting to the motion of the boat. The familiar motion.

Familiar? What did he know about boats? Not much. But Travis did.

I'll leave you alone now, the other consciousness inside his brain said.

How could Travis ever leave him alone? He was here with him. He struggled to work that out, but the effort to slog his way through it was currently too much.

He was holding Olivia's hand, clinging to her as if she could make sense of everything for him. Vaguely, he knew there were things he should say to her, but he wasn't sure they were the right things. He wasn't sure what to worry about first. His relationship with her? Or his relationship with his life? Was he still a Decorah agent, or what? At the moment, it was all too much. He would have to make sense of everything later. Right now, he couldn't even cling to consciousness.

CHAPTER TWENTY-THREE

Gabe woke with a start when the boat bumped against a pier. Olivia was no longer beside him. She was talking to one of the women—the one he knew was called Rachel.

He heard her say, "It has to be confusing for him. Give him some time."

Olivia nodded, and he sensed that she was making an effort to give him some space.

Good. Because he needed it.

He sat up and looked around, seeing that they were at the public dock in the center of St. Stephens.

One of the men came over and gave him a critical look. "How are you feeling?"

He considered the question. Somewhere in his mind, he heard the word, "Reborn." But instead of saying that, he answered, "Okay."

"Good. You remember who we are?"

"Dr. Solomon's experiments."

"Yeah. I'm Jake."

The others circled him and introduced themselves. He sorted them out and put them into couples. That part was pretty obvious because of the bond between them. Jake and Rachel. Stephanie and Craig. Matt and Elizabeth.

And he and Olivia. Was he like them now? He wasn't sure.

Jake and Matt helped him off the boat and into a rental van.

Apparently, they'd made plans while he was asleep, because their next stop was a discount department store.

The couple, Craig and Stephanie, went to buy dry clothes for everyone who had been in the water, and some other necessities for Gabe and Olivia.

While they were in the store, Jake came back to him. "Do you know a small, out-of-the-way motel where we could spend the night and make some plans?"

Gabe realized that he did. "The Driftwood."

Jake used his phone to check the location and then to make a reservation for the group.

Matt registered everybody and collected the keys. Gabe had a room to himself, and he was steady enough to take a shower on his own.

He had just finished combing his hair when he heard a knock at the door. When he opened it, he found Olivia standing there.

"Can I come in?"

He stepped aside, and she entered, carefully closing the door behind her.

He remembered on the boat, Travis saying that he would leave him alone, but now Gabe felt the other man again and felt his emotions. He found himself looking at Olivia with a hunger that he felt light up every cell of his body. It was an unexpected jolt. He'd been attracted to her, sure. But this new emotion was a shock to his soul. It was Travis's hunger, and somehow it was his own as well, because he was as much Travis Carson as Gabe Bowman.

Still unable to focus on what that might mean on a personal level, he grabbed for a less fraught topic—Travis's work. He had made his life on the water, and Gabe knew nothing about boats. Or did he?

Yes. Suddenly, it was all there. All the knowledge he had lacked. He knew all the working parts of a boat. All the things you had to do to maintain a safe and seaworthy vessel. The price of marine fuel. Navigational markers. What to do in a storm. How to prepare his boat for the winter.

He didn't have to ask questions about the subject. The knowledge was just *there* like someone had dumped it all into his brain. Or to put it another way—like something he had always known.

His legs had gone wobbly, and he took a step to the side so that he could prop a shoulder against the wall.

Olivia stayed where she was, her gaze alert and worried. "Are you okay?"

"I don't know." He dragged in a breath and let it out. Part of him wanted to reach for her. The other part wanted to be alone while he sorted out what he was now.

He looked down at his hand, a hand he recognized. Turning it slightly, he found the scar he'd gotten when he'd crashed into a brick wall on his skateboard. "I'm Gabe. And I'm also Travis," he said in a shaky voice, testing the knowledge as he said the words aloud.

She silently nodded.

"And you know."

"Yes."

A piece of newly acquired knowledge tumbled out of him. "His father never forgave him for killing his mom when he was born."

"Yes."

"He was lonely all his life, until he met you."

"I was just as lonely," she answered.

The enormity of his situation started to kick in. He was himself—Gabe Bowman, the person he had always been. But he was also Travis Carson.

"How am I supposed to deal with all of that?"

He wasn't sure what emotion he read on her face. Hope? Doubt? Fear of the unknown?

"You could let me help you," she answered. "Or—we could help each other."

When she stepped forward, he stayed where he was. He had watched her and Travis and thought how lucky the guy was to have her. But that was before he was forced to deal with his new truth.

When her arms came up to wrap around him, he stood rigidly for a moment before letting himself relax into her embrace.

As she gathered him to her, he knew that he wasn't just the fusion of two men. One of them was bonded to the woman who held him in her arms. He could talk to her without saying any words aloud. Could Gabe do it too? As a test, he said, *You could have been talking to me inside my head when you first came in.*

Yes.

Why didn't you?

I didn't want to push you into anything...unfamiliar. I know you need to ease into it.

His body shuddered. Whether he was ready for it or not, it was here.

She didn't move, only held him, and his own arms came up to clasp her. She was offering him comfort and a whole lot more.

Before he could take that reality any further, a knock at the door startled them both, and they sprang apart. Gabe ran a hand through his hair, and Olivia pulled at the hem of her T-shirt.

When Gabe opened the door, Jake was standing on the walkway outside.

His expression was apologetic as he said, "Sorry to interrupt, but Rachel needs to talk to Travis."

Gabe goggled at him. "Talk to Travis," he repeated.

"We need his help—uh, your help," Jake clarified.

"With what?"

"Gabe and Olivia were unconscious when the boat left the dock. Travis was the only one awake. Rachel thinks he can tell us where to find Smith. He's harmed a lot of us—

not just you two. Maybe he even got some of us killed. If we can shut him down, we can keep him from going after anyone else."

Gabe felt a ripple of excitement. It was followed by a jolt of fear. He flashed back to the room where he'd been held—and to what Smith had done to Olivia and Travis. He'd vowed to make the bastard pay. Jake and the others were just as anxious to put an end to Smith's obsession with Dr. Solomon's experiments. Now he had the chance to make good on his vow.

"Okay, what do you need from me?"

"Come down to our room."

He glanced at Olivia.

"I'm coming too," she said.

"Of course," Jake answered.

They both followed him along the concrete strip fronting the motel. Rachel and Jake's quarters were larger than his and apparently being used as a sort of headquarters. The rest of the rescue group was already there, sitting on extra chairs arranged in a circle.

Gabe stopped short. He'd been asked here to talk to Rachel. It seemed it wasn't just her.

When all eyes turned to him, he felt suddenly awkward. The star attraction in an impromptu reality show. Probably they were all wondering how his...transition was going. At least nobody asked any direct questions.

He scuffed a foot against the worn carpet. "I should thank you for saving my life."

"Travis did it," Rachel said, perhaps reminding him why he was standing there.

Olivia jumped into the conversation. "But both of us would be dead if you hadn't flown halfway across the country, rented a boat, and come after Smith's men."

Gabe nodded in acknowledgement. "What do you need me to do?"

Rachel gestured toward an empty chair. "Sit down and get comfortable."

He was thinking, *with a bunch of people staring at me.*

But the others must have picked up the thought because Craig said, "Why don't we give you some space?"

He got up and went into the adjoining room. Everyone but Olivia followed. She looked at him and asked in a not-quite-steady voice," Can I stay?"

"Sure," he said, not because he wanted her to but because he suspected he was too open to her for it to make any difference whether she stayed or went.

Rachel nodded. *We can teach you how to shield your thoughts,* she silently told him. "But now we've got urgent business. Smith could decide that his current location is too hot and clear out. We want to get him before he does."

"So what do I do?" he asked.

Just chill out, she answered in his mind. Her next remark was addressed to Travis. *When Smith first brought you to his house, it was by boat. And you left the same way. Could you recognize the dock?*

He felt Travis's hesitation, and he had the strange

feeling that the other man was maybe asking permission to speak.

Go ahead, Gabe said.

Thanks.

He felt the word form in his own mind, and he tried to stay calm, tried to accept that he was now two people—who weren't exactly comfortable with each other. Could he really cope with this...duality?

Rachel waited through the silent exchange before saying, *You've already proved you're strong—and adaptable.*

How do you know? he shot back.

Because I can see you dealing with it. But we're not here for a Tarot card reading. I need facts.

That was the first time he realized that reading the cards was Rachel's profession. He had always thought that fortune-telling was a bunch of hooey. This woman could change his mind. She'd said he was strong. He sensed that in her as well.

His musings were cut off when Travis began to speak. *I think so. I was trying to mark where it was so we could come back. If we got a chance,* he added with a dull, angry note in his silent voice, and Gabe knew that Rachel picked it up.

You thought it might be a one-way trip.

Yeah. But I was hoping you might get here in time to make a difference. I know what the back of the house looks like. It's got to be on the Miles River. That's the main waterway leading from the bay to St. Stephens. That's how I take my boat to open water. I'd seen the house a thousand times. I don't know how long it's belonged to Smith.

A picture of a large gray stone mansion came into his mind. It was a two-story house with a portico that ran along the back. Outdoor furniture was arranged in conversational groupings along its length. And closer to the water, there was a gazebo with a blue roof. The shoreline along the water had been reinforced with more gray rocks, larger and more jagged than the ones from which the house was built. The pier was about thirty feet long. A sleek speedboat was moored along the left side.

Getaway boat? Rachel mused. *I guess we have to cover the front and the back. What can you tell me about the interior of the house?*

Normal-looking living room, dining room, and kitchen along the water. The coercion facilities are in the left wing.

Again, there were all too clear mental pictures of the room where Travis and Olivia had been tortured and the cell where Gabe had been held in the basement.

Okay, let's look for the place on Google Maps, Rachel said. *Then we can plan an invasion with one assault team coming in by boat and another by car. How many henchmen does he have?*

I've seen six different men including the ones who captured us at Olivia's house. I don't know how many will be there at any given time. Maybe it depends on how relaxed Smith is feeling now that he thinks he's gotten rid of a major threat.

Or maybe he keeps several guards on duty at all times,

Rachel put in. *Thanks. I think we've got what we need. And now we'd better get busy.* "I'm going to call in the others for a tactical meeting." She gave Gabe and Olivia a critical look. "The two of you almost drowned a few hours ago. Are you in shape for a raid tonight?"

"Yes," they both answered.

"I'd give you more time to recuperate, but I don't want to give Smith a chance to slip away," Rachel added.

Gabe stood up and stretched, testing his muscles. He'd automatically answered her question in the affirmative, but he wasn't exactly in prime shape. Still, he agreed with Rachel. "Yeah. The sooner we deal with the bastard, the better."

In fact, he was glad that he didn't have to sit around his room stewing over his newfound double personality. Or figuring out how to deal with Olivia. Probably she caught that thought, but there was nothing he could do about anything personal between them at the moment.

CHAPTER TWENTY-FOUR

The rest of the group came back for a planning session. First, they called up Google Maps on a laptop that was Bluetoothed to the room's TV. Using Travis's memory of Olivia and Gabe being carried from the house, they found a river view of the property. From there, they moved the map to the street side. No surprise that the estate was on River Road, along with a slew of other mansions. All were on large lots, which meant less chance of disturbing the neighbors. Before they got down to a tactical discussion, Jake said, "We should tell Olivia and Gabe our skills, and find out what they can do."

Gabe was about to say he couldn't do any mental tricks, when he felt an odd sensation like electricity buzzing through his body. His gaze shot to Olivia.

I'm feeding you energy, she silently told him.

He gave a small nod of acknowledgement, wondering

if what she was doing could have any practical effect on him.

Yes, Travis answered.

Before he had time to dwell on the strangeness of the interchange, he somehow felt Olivia directing his focus toward a plastic cup on the bathroom counter.

To his shock, the vessel went skittering off the sink counter onto the floor.

While he was marveling at that new talent, Olivia reminded him of what happened during his stealthy approach to her estate.

"We can also hurl what we're calling thunderbolts," she said, giving him a pointed look. Well, she and Travis had. Not him. Travis had thought the man sneaking up on them was an attacker and had zapped him unconscious.

You think...I can do that? he challenged.

Yes. But we'd better not do it in here. When she walked to the door, he followed slowly, wondering if she could possibly be right.

When he looked around for witnesses, Jake said, "I rented the whole motel. There are no other guests. And Gabe and Elizabeth sent the guy in the office a strong suggestion to turn on the No Vacancy sign and go home. He's cleared out."

"You can do that?"

"Yes. Some of us are better at it than others," Craig put in. "I did a lot of it when I rescued Stephanie from the scumbag who thought he was going to marry her."

Actually, I think I got Smith focused on drowning you

—rather than getting rid of you in a fiery car crash, Travis added.

Gabe winced, then tensed when Olivia came up behind him and clasped him around the waist—making him flash on her and Travis practicing their defenses back at her estate.

After looking around to make sure no cars were coming up the road, she fed him energy, and they sent a jolt into a metal trash container near the Coke machine, making the container jump.

"I'll be damned," Gabe muttered.

Too bad we don't have time—or a good place—for more practice, she answered.

He grinned, pleased to have exhibited some of the power that the others now took for granted. Would he ever feel entirely comfortable with them? For that matter, would he ever feel entirely comfortable in his own skin? He couldn't answer that yet. First, they had to deal with the man who had tried to kill them.

"Good job," Jake said. "Now we should share our talents with you."

Back inside, the couples filled in the newcomers on what they'd been able to accomplish. They all had mastered thunderbolts. Craig, Elizabeth, and Matt were particularly good at mind control.

And as a group, they were much more powerful—like when they'd hidden their vessel while approaching Smith's murder boat.

As Gabe had suspected, Rachel was the most talented

of the group. He learned that she'd saved her own life, plus Jake's and the two members of the group that he hadn't met yet, Gabriella and Luke. She'd slowed down time when Dr. Solomon had blown up his own laboratory after Rachel and Jake had come to rescue the other two telepaths.

When everyone had catalogued their abilities, they got down to serious planning, with Gabe and Craig, the two detectives, providing the major input.

"We can't be sure how this will go down," Craig cautioned everyone. "You have to be prepared to change plans in the middle of the action if your assumptions blow up in your face. When I rescued Stephanie from her fiancé's wedding farce, I was going to wait until the guests were all seated before trying to get out of there. But one of his men found the guard I'd tied up and left in the bushes, and I had to seriously move up the timetable."

Gabe wanted to hear more of *that* story. But he knew it would have to wait until there were no more threats hanging over their heads.

Switching gears, he said, "Besides your hidden talents, we've got an interesting advantage."

They all turned expectantly to him.

"Smith sent his men out to deep-six me and Olivia. He has no reason to suspect that we survived being tossed overboard with weights around our ankles. How's he going to react when he sees us invade his property?"

"I think he was already worried about Travis's ghost— and fearful of what he considered our supernatural powers," Olivia added with a hitch in her voice. "Maybe seeing us again will give him the scare of his life."

"An excellent angle," Jake said. "Just don't get overconfident about playing ghosts. He might have some tricks up his sleeve you don't know about."

Olivia cleared her throat, and everyone turned toward her. "Smith struck me as the kind of guy who doesn't take chances. I mean, he kept drugging me when somebody else wouldn't have thought it necessary. She paused before blurting out, "I wish we had some idea of what defenses he has. He could hit us with something we haven't taken into consideration."

"Good point." Rachel nodded and turned to Gabe but was clearly addressing Travis. "You were able to move through the house unseen. Did you see anything we have to worry about?"

As he was learning to do, Gabe mentally stepped back and let his alter ego do the talking. "I saw a control room with a lot of screens. A man was always on duty watching them. He's got views all over the property. Including the boat dock."

"I was prepared for that," Craig answered. "We have to disable the exterior cameras when we come in. Anything else?"

"He also had a lot of electronic equipment. I don't know what that was for. I suppose it could be for communications. But electronics isn't my field. It could be something dangerous to us."

"I don't like it," Jake mused.

"Remember his trick with the football helmets," Matt added.

"Which is?" Olivia asked.

Matt laughed. "You know those old jokes about mental patients shielding their brains with tin foil? He took it to heart and lined helmets with aluminum foil. Unfortunately, we couldn't get any mental suggestions through to his men when they were wearing them."

Elizabeth nodded. "If they have on helmets, we'll have to assume we can't influence them."

They went on to speculate about what defenses Smith might have ginned up against an invasion of psychics. But nobody had a definitive answer.

Finally, Jake cut off the planning session. "Again, we can't be ready for every contingency. But I do know we should have a meal before we head for Smith's place." He gave Olivia and Gabe a considering look. "The two of you have to stay out of sight on the off chance that Smith or one of his men would recognize you. I'll go into town and pick up some food." He turned to Gabe, "You're the only one from around here. Where's the best place to get something quick and good?"

Gabe tensed in confusion. He wasn't from around here. He was from Silver Spring.

Okay for me to answer? Travis questioned inside his head.

Sure. As he replied, he was wondering if the two personalities inside his brain would ever mold themselves into one.

"The Crab Claw, down by the downtown dock," he told Jake.

"Thanks—let's look at the online menu, and we can place an order."

While the members of the group were making selections, Travis said inside Gabe's head, *This isn't The Invasion of the Body Snatchers.*

What is it?

I don't know yet, but I'm hoping we can...get comfortable with each other.

Could they?

If not, Gabe was afraid he was going to end up in a mental hospital. Maybe he could be a unique case study and make some psychiatrist famous.

The private conversation was interrupted by Jake asking for their order.

Crab cakes okay? Travis asked.

Yeah. And onion rings.

Perfect.

Jake looked over at Craig, "Why don't you drive me into town. I'll pick up a second vehicle while you go down to the dock and rent a cabin cruiser."

"And you'll both use false IDs and make sure that whoever handles the transactions can't remember who you are," Rachel added.

"Right," they both answered.

Jake looked at Craig. "Then you come back here while I pick up the food." He switched his attention to the others, "And while we're away, the rest of you get some rest."

OLIVIA WAS glad to return to her room and lie down. She was feeling like her nerves were crawling out of her skin. And the attack of uncertainty wasn't just about confronting the man who'd captured and tortured her.

Although she'd never admitted it, she'd always been lonely until Travis had pushed his way into her life. No one else would be able to understand what they'd had together. Well, the others had the same kind of special bond, but nobody else had experienced their unique relationship. Now that had been obliterated. Travis was still here—in a way, but the intensity of what they'd shared was gone.

Everything that had happened with him flooded back to her. When she'd first felt his presence, she'd been afraid of him. Then they'd come to some kind of uneasy accommodation. That had turned into a deep need, each for the other. As the relationship had progressed, they'd grown closer and closer. He'd been able to—she wasn't sure what to call it. Attach himself to her? Live through her? It was far from ordinary. And it certainly wasn't ideal to have a lover nobody else could see or hear. But it had worked for them. They'd been as close as two people could be. He'd come to be within instant reach. And he'd helped save her from drowning.

When he'd said he could also save Gabe, she'd urged him to do it. He'd warned her that Gabe would never be the same. And he wouldn't either. She hadn't known what that would mean, but she'd desperately wanted Gabe to live, because his only crime had been helping her find Travis's killer. In the urgency of the moment, there hadn't been time for explanations. Maybe even Travis hadn't known what was going to happen. But when he'd brought Gabe back to life, everything had changed.

Instead of being attached to her, Travis was now part of Gabe. That had to be a good thing. He was no longer dead. He was a living, breathing man again—as part of Gabe. But could the two men happily exist in the same body? Would the transformation be too much for them? She didn't know, and she was sure they didn't either.

From observing the other couples forged from Dr. Solomon's experiments, she could see what she had lost. They were all so close. And now she was cut off from her soulmate. Even though he was right here.

A wave of deep sadness swept through her. She could never get back the closeness of having Travis with her the way he had been. That was gone forever. He was now part of Gabe Bowman, a man who probably hated having a parasite attached to him. Was that how he thought about Travis? Or would he come to see the other man as value added?

She laughed bitterly. Maybe her newfound happiness was over before it had had a chance to really take root.

Could she and Gabe/Travis forge something else together?

There was no way to formulate an answer yet.

Having come to no firm conclusions, she tried to sleep, but her mind was still churning too much for her to relax.

It was almost a relief when Jake and Craig came back, and the group pulled a couple of tables together so they could eat in one room.

She watched the couples automatically choose seats next to each other, leaving two adjoining chairs for her and Gabe.

She gave him a shy look. As far as the group was concerned, they were paired up, yet they weren't the same as everyone else.

She watched Jake, who owned a restaurant in New Orleans, take a bite from a crab cake sandwich and chew. "Different from our seafood style," he announced.

"Trust you to critique the food," Rachel teased, her remark slicing through the tension they were all feeling.

"Gabriella would do it too—if she were here," Jake answered in mock defense.

Olivia supposed he and Rachel were trying for normality. But it wasn't quite working.

GABE FELT guilty as he tried to choke down some crab cake and onion rings. He knew this was the first food Travis had eaten since Smith had captured him, and he wasn't letting the guy enjoy his dinner.

Sorry.

We'll both feel more like eating when this operation is over.

He'd managed to finish half the crab cake and most of his onion rings when Craig brought them all back to business.

He put down his sandwich and said, "I've set up two teams. One for the land approach and the other by the river. Gabe and Olivia, Elizabeth, and Matt will be Team A—coming in by water, since..." he stopped and looked abashed for a moment. "Since Travis knows the river."

"Makes sense," Gabe said.

Since the trip was shorter by road, team B, consisting of Rachel, Jake, Craig, and Stephanie, would wait at the motel until the boat was on its way to Smith's mansion. This would also give them a chance to make sure telepathic communication between the teams was working.

After eating, they packed up and put all their clothing and equipment into the SUV.

Before leaving, they wiped every surface in the motel that they had touched, and took their trash to a dumpster a couple of miles away.

They set out on the mission not long after dark. There were few boats on the river, but Gabe did see some marine lights in the channel.

He watched Olivia, Matt, and Elizabeth standing beside him in the wheelhouse.

"We've got communication with the other team," she announced.

"Good."

"We'll keep checking in."

"Okay," Gabe answered. He didn't have a big role in the communications. He was still too new to talk mind-to-mind over any distance. But he marveled that he was the captain of the A Team. Although he was the new guy in the group, Travis had made his living on the water. He was the one who had the knowledge of the river and the properties along the bank. He was also the one who had the most to fear. He knew from firsthand experience that Smith had more tricks up his sleeve than the others could imagine.

CHAPTER TWENTY-FIVE

Harold Goddard, alias Mr. Smith, walked restlessly around the first floor of his mansion.

He had nothing to worry about, he told himself. He'd killed three people in the past few days, and that should take care of any problems he could anticipate. First, there had been the boat captain, Carson. Then the detective, Gabe Bowman, and the artist, Olivia Langston. Both of the latter had been stupid to get tangled up in his business.

Now they were all dead. That should put an end to any worries he had. But he couldn't rein in his paranoia. Only it wasn't paranoia if you really did think someone could be stalking you.

He stopped in the control room and saw that Andrew was watching the screens. When Harold saw nothing unusual, he went out back and scanned the river. It was quiet and peaceful in the darkness. But far in the distance, he saw the lights of a boat. As he watched, they winked off.

Or was that a trick of his mind? Had he really seen a boat disable its lights in the navigation channel? And if he was right, did that mean an invasion force was coming for him? If so, who the hell were they and how did they know to show up here?

Conspiracy theories swirled in his head, but he had to ignore them for the moment. If he was under attack, he had to defend himself.

He rushed back to the control room in time to see an SUV on the camera that monitored traffic on River Road. It slowed when it passed his driveway, then continued out of sight. Nothing usual except the slowing, but his fine-tuned sense of worry had begun to make his nerve endings tingle.

"Let me take the chair," he said abruptly.

Andrew stood at once and moved to the side of the room. Harold quickly slid into the seat. He'd been preparing himself for trouble since he'd first taken over this estate. He'd put special measures in place. Too bad that some of them were untested. But there were others that depended on good old-fashioned armament.

First, he sent out a vibrating alarm to the phone of each of the guards on duty, cursing himself that he'd given some of them the evening off.

When he had alerted the men, he reached to pull out the computer keyboard and began to call up a program.

As he worked, he split his attention between the computer and the man standing beside him.

"Get to the front of the house," he said. "And be prepared to execute the drill we practiced."

"Yes, sir." As his henchman answered, he was already on his way out the door.

———

RACHEL WAS in the shotgun seat beside Jake as he slowed on River Road.

"I think we'd better get a few hundred feet from the mansion before we park," he said.

There were murmurs of agreement from Stephanie and Craig behind them.

Jake found a place where he could pull off the road. After he parked, Rachel sent a message to the team in the boat. *We're here.*

Reading you loud and clear, Matt sent back.

Where are you?

Approaching the dock at low power.

We'll get in position near the front door.

So far, so good.

As soon as we spot the cameras, I'm going to cut the power to the surveillance system, including the lights, Rachel said. *That will probably alert Smith that something's up. But on balance, it's better that he can't see us.*

Matt sent her his agreement. They had discussed cloaking themselves psychically, the way they had when they'd mounted the water rescue mission. But in the end, they'd decided that making themselves invisible would drain away too much power with the group, so spread out.

The foursome got out of the vehicle, collected the weapons they'd brought, and started back to the mansion on foot, moving as silently as they could through the darkness, staying off the road, keeping to cover as much as possible.

As they drew near Smith's property, Jake scanned the roofline of the house and the trees.

I see the cameras, he informed them, directing the others to the locations.

They all stopped, formed into a tight group, and sent energy to Rachel as she shorted out the video system. In the next moment, she cried out as something she had never experienced jolted her. She couldn't say what it was, but all at once some kind of bolt struck her. Not something physical. It was mental, and it shot straight to her brain. Her hands went to her head as she tried to block out the intense pain that bloomed like a nuclear explosion. The others in the group gasped, and she knew they were experiencing the same sensation.

It was impossible to stay on her feet. Her knees buckled, and she fell to the side, hitting Stephanie on the way down.

*Smith must have...*she tried to say, but she couldn't form the words.

It had happened fast, and it had happened to all of them. And there was more than pain. She felt a grogginess invading her mind like mist creeping along the ground swallowing up the landscape.

To her amazement, when she looked up, she saw that Jake was still standing. She tried to reach him with her mind, but for the first time since they'd bonded, that was impossible. She simply couldn't catch his thoughts.

Fear crackled inside her, and she realized how much she'd come to depend on that mental connection. It was as though she had lost part of herself. Was it the same for him?

She felt his hand find hers and squeeze. "Gotta get out of here," he croaked.

"I...can't."

"You have to," he said, giving a savage tug on her arm. "Or we're gonna die." Somehow the tug and the words prodded her to action.

She might not be able to stand. She might not be able to think clearly. But if she had any say in the matter, she wasn't going to let Smith wipe her out—along with the rest of her clan. She began to crawl away from the house, back toward the road, praying she could escape from whatever was turning her mind to cottage cheese.

Anxiously, she spared a glance back over her shoulder and thanked God that Craig and Stephanie were following. They looked as bad as she felt, but they were moving. As she fought through air that had turned to thick syrup around her, she remembered something else that froze the blood in her veins. The boat team was headed for the dock. She had to stop them. Desperately she tried to send a message, but she couldn't get the words out past the invisible wall around her head.

GABE GUIDED the boat silently toward the pier that jutted out into the water.

It was like his mind was divided into two halves. Travis focused on the navigation and Gabe scanned the estate ahead, where floodlights illuminated the grounds. He could see no guards on duty, but he knew the surroundings were under observation. Probably there was a man in the control room he'd seen sitting at the bank of screens watching for trouble. How many men were there besides Smith?

He'd seen six. There could be more.

When the exterior went dark, he knew that the other team had cut the outside power. Presumably, that meant that not only were the spots out but also the video cameras.

Beside him, Matt sent his thanks to Rachel.

Immediately, he sensed trouble.

"Rachel didn't answer," Matt informed him.

At the words, a knot of worry started deep in his chest. There was a time when Travis could have flitted to the front of the house to find out what was going on out there. Those days were over.

As soon as the boat bumped against a piling, Matt snatched up a knapsack, jumped out, and began tying up the vessel. The moment it was secure, he turned and helped Elizabeth out. Olivia stayed by Gabe's side.

Gabe was halfway to the lawn when he heard Travis shouting inside his head. Not just to him but to the other members of the water team.

Get off the dock. Get off the dock.

Could they jump into the water?

No. They had already reached the bulwark of large, jagged rocks that reinforced the shoreline.

All he could do was throw down his pack, grab Olivia's hand, and run toward land, pulling her after him. Together, they pounded up the last few feet of boards behind Matt and Elizabeth, who had already made it to the lawn and were heading for cover behind a gazebo.

He and Olivia were seconds behind them. They had almost reached the other two team members when he felt the ground shake. Moments later, he heard an enormous boom behind him, like a barrage of artillery shells had gone off. He grabbed Olivia and pulled her down, covering her body with his as debris from the pier and the boat began to shower down. Wood and metal flew through the air like confetti, and Gabe braced for impact. But everybody else was focused on protection. He could feel himself and Olivia joining with Matt and Elizabeth to put up a dome over the four of them. As the deadly rain fell, it was deflected, bouncing off the invisible shield, preventing anything from hitting them. When one of the boat's twin engines landed nearby, he shuddered.

He eased off Olivia, but cradled her against him,

thankful that she was all right, vividly aware that he could have lost her in these first moments of the invasion.

I wish you hadn't come. The silent words were from Travis.

I go where you do, she answered.

He couldn't stop trembling, and he knew it wasn't fear for himself. It was fear for her.

Whose emotions am I feeling, yours or mine? he asked the other man who had joined with him in his body.

Does it matter?

He could only answer, *No.*

But he knew this was not the time for a philosophical discussion. They had to save their lives—and get to Smith. The bastard had already proved he was tricky. This was just more evidence of his relentless ability to counter threats.

Gabe wasn't sure how long they lay there, but finally, the immediate effects of the blast subsided.

How did you know? he asked Travis.

I can't explain it, even to myself. I was on alert for the bastard to do something totally unexpected. Then I sensed it.

We'd all be dead if you hadn't warned us, Matt said.

Or seriously injured if you hadn't put up that shield.

You were part of it.

Can we assume Smith thinks he sent us to our maker? Elizabeth asked.

Assume nothing, Gabe shot back. *We have to get to a more secure location. Men could be coming to investigate.*

Stay low. Stay in the shadows. Somewhere in his mind, he realized he was silently speaking to the others with sudden ease. He guessed that the emergency had juiced up his ability.

After weighing the pros and cons of staying together or splitting up, he decided that separating only gave the enemy the opportunity to pick them off one by one.

I'm going to contact the other team, Matt said.

Gabe waited tensely for word that Rachel and the other four were okay. When Matt shook his head, Gabe felt the terrible tension in his chest expand. What the hell had happened to Rachel's team?

Or were they somehow being blocked from responding? He prayed it was that simple. At least he hadn't heard another explosion—or gunfire.

CHAPTER TWENTY-SIX

Rachel kept crawling away from the mansion. Blacktop stretched in front of her. Was it taking too much of a chance to cross the road? If a car came, they were done for. But getting to the other side of the country lane might be the only way to cut off the effects of whatever device Smith was using on them.

When she heard an explosion, she felt a stab of alarm. What was that? Had Smith set a trap for the other team? Not the same thing as this, but something more immediately deadly.

She turned her head toward Jake and saw him force words out of his mouth.

"Keep going."

She glanced down the road, then reached to put a hand on the blacktop. It was still warm from the day's heat. Summoning an image of the Tarot Wheel of Fortune, she struggled to block out danger. But tonight the card failed her. When she was halfway across the black-top, she saw headlights bearing down on her. Teeth clenched, she tried to move faster, but it was no good. Her body was too weakened by whatever Smith had thrown at them. There was simply no chance she could get out of the way in time. The headlights came closer, blinding her. Didn't the driver see that there was someone on the pavement?

The vehicle was almost on top of her when she felt a strong arm grasp her and scoop her up. Jake pulled her to safety just as the car sped over the spot where she had been lying moments earlier.

She flopped to the gravel of the shoulder, gasping. Beside her, she could hear Jake's breath sawing in and out of his lungs. She had lost track of him on the endless trip across what had seemed like a continent's worth of pavement. But he had known where *she* was, and he had saved her.

She had feared that whatever device Smith had used would cause them permanent damage. But as they lay limply on the shoulder, she began to feel her body returning to normal. And as she'd hoped, Smith's psychic defense shield only extended to the road. Once they were out of range, they were free of the effects.

Sitting up, she looked across and saw Craig and Stephanie still sprawled on the far side of the divide.

She cupped her hands and called across. "Stay on that side, and we'll get you."

"Get as close to the road as you can," Jake added.

She and her soulmate both stood. *Can you hear me now?* She silently asked.

Yes.

Thank God.

How about—you grab Craig, and I'll grab Stephanie.

They were about to dash the way they'd come when a loud pop alerted them to a gunman nearby.

They both dropped to the ground. Looking up, Rachel saw a man running forward, firing as he charged toward Craig and Stephanie.

When they'd been on the other side of the road, Rachel and Jake had hardly been able to move. But her powers were coming back to her.

Centering herself, she tried to pull together enough power to do some damage. As she readied herself to hurl an energy bolt, she felt Jake sending her power. When the man with the gun spotted them, he swiveled the gun in their direction. Before he could fire, she sent the bolt into his chest. A look of surprise bloomed on his face, and he staggered but held onto the weapon. Knowing she had to put out more power, she gathered everything she had and struck him again. This time, he fell to the ground and went limp.

Was he still a threat? She couldn't be sure, and she couldn't expend the energy to find out. If she was going to cross to the tainted side of the road, it must be for one purpose only—to pull the other members of the team to safety.

She glanced at Jake and caught his agreement. They were

about to go back to their original plan when the headlights of another car cut through the darkness. They waited for it to pass before charging back across the road. Immediately, she felt the debilitating effects of whatever anti-psychic force Smith was using. But this time she was ready for it and had a better idea how to shield herself. Nevertheless, it was almost impossible to pull Stephanie out of danger while staying on her feet.

She managed to do it because she had to. But she was wobbling on shaky legs by the time she made it across to the safe side of the blacktop.

She wanted to flop down, but she forced herself to keep going, and put more distance between themselves and any more guards who might come charging out of the house.

He only sent one guy, which means he's short on help, Jake observed.

And that guy's out of commission.

How many more does he have?

I'd like to know.

Beside her, Stephanie made a small sound, and Rachel looked down at her friend. In the dim light, she saw a dark stain on the left sleeve of her shirt.

"You're hit," she gasped.

Craig answered with a low curse and was immediately at his soulmate's side, rolling up her sleeve.

She winced.

Sorry. I've got to find out the damage. After a careful inspection, he said, *It looks like a through and through.*

"And you're unhurt," Jake demanded.

"Yeah." Craig was already opening the medical kit they'd brought and pulling out gauze. He slathered it with antiseptics and pressed it to Stephanie's arm.

When she gasped, he apologized again

"It's not so bad," she assured him, before he secured the field dressing with a gauze strip.

The four attackers stayed hunkered down in the woods.

"We obviously didn't expect a defense quite so sophisticated," Jake muttered. "I wonder what's happening with the other team."

"There was a big explosion," Craig said. "Let's hope they're okay. We're supposed to be helping them," he added, "but unless something changes, we can't even get across the street."

"What if we don't try to go directly across? We can keep walking on this side until we find out where it's possible to cross," Rachel answered. "Then we have to work our way back and hope he doesn't have the same kind of setup at the rear of the house."

"Why would you assume he doesn't?" Stephanie asked.

"Because we heard that explosion. If he needed to blow something up, that means he didn't think he could stop them the same way he stopped us," Jake answered.

The explanation made sense, and Rachel prayed that it was true.

GABE and the three others who had been in the boat were still on the ground. "Everyone okay?" he asked.

One by one, they checked in. The shield had worked. There were no injuries.

When they dissolved the bubble, smoke drifted in around them, and he could hear everyone struggling not to cough.

"We've got to move and we've got to find shelter before he figures out the explosion didn't get us."

Switch to silent communications, Travis said.

Sorry, I...heard your warning, but I'm not so sure of myself with this mind-to-mind stuff.

Travis interrupted the other man sharing a body with him. *I know you're not used to it. Okay if I do it for you?*

Fine.

Matt spoke. *I remember the aerial Google view. There's some kind of small structure up along the slope.*

Gabe let Travis convey his thought. *Let's head for it. But be careful. I heard gunfire from the other side of the house. Someone must have been shooting at the road team.*

I hope they could return fire with a mental blast, Elizabeth said.

They stayed low and silent as they moved up the hill. Gabe also remembered the small structure, but they had landed before he got a chance to orient himself to the property. And the smoke wasn't helping. Unfortunately, he couldn't be sure where they were going.

Olivia was the one who found the small building. As an artist, she had good spatial visualization, and she silently directed them to the right. They came to a small structure that stuck out from the hill. There was no wall on the front, but an iron gate barred the way to the interior.

Gabe looked up the hill, seeing the beams of three flashlights coming from the house.

They're on their way to investigate, he silently told the others.

On it, Matt answered.

He, Elizabeth, and Olivia had formed a unit. They were doing something to the gate that Gabe couldn't see.

As the lights drew closer, he sidestepped to the front of the building where the others were gathered. He heard the gate creak as it swung to the side. The rest of the group moved quickly inside. The interior space was small and dank, but they managed to cram in, just as a beam of light reached the side of the building.

The barrier was already back in place, and the lights continued down the hill, all except one, which swung to the bars behind which they crouched.

As the light played over the opening, a hand reached out to try and rattle the gate.

Somehow it held fast.

Satisfied that nobody was inside, the searcher moved on, and Gabe let out the breath he was holding.

How did you pull that off? he asked, using the silent voice he had acquired so recently. *I mean, why didn't he see us when he looked through?*

I painted him a blank canvas, Olivia answered.

And we held the gate in place with our minds, Elizabeth added.

She abruptly went silent because the men outside were speaking. They all sounded tough but also wary.

"See anything?"

"The dock is gone. So is any boat that landed."

"If there was a boat."

"Smith said he saw one coming."

"I hope he didn't destroy his dock for nothing." There was a pause. "Wait a minute. There *was* a boat, and I see parts of it scattered around."

"Any body parts?"

"Not so far as I can tell. But I don't know how anybody on the boat could have survived that blast.

The light beams moved around on the grass.

"There's a strange debris pattern here."

"What do you mean?"

"See this circle? It's totally clear."

"Which means what?"

"It's like someone put up a huge, iron umbrella to keep the stuff from falling on them."

"Oh, come on."

"Look for yourself. How do you explain it?"

"I can't," another man snapped.

"We'd better spread out and make sure nobody got away."

As Gabe watched, the trio move apart. One of the men went to the right. The other to the left. The two of them disappeared from sight, but the third came back toward the little structure where the invaders were hiding.

When Gabe saw his face in the moonlight, the hairs on his arms began to prickle, and his skin tightened.

It's Lambert, one of the bastards who chartered my boat like they were coming out for a day of fun on the water.

One of the same guys who put the weights on Olivia and me before throwing us overboard, Gabe added.

He had always prided himself on his ability to keep cool. Now the silent conversation was building up pressure in his chest that would have to explode or kill him.

He and Travis were in perfect accord—each of them feeding the other's anger. This was one of the thugs who had killed them. And here was the perfect opportunity to even the score.

Some part of Gabe recognized that he was being reckless—that *they* were being reckless. But there was no way to pull back the tide of murderous rage surging inside him —inside them.

He felt Olivia's hand on his arm.

Don't. The voice of reason. Yet he couldn't listen to her.

Before he fully realized what he was doing, he blew the gate off the entrance to the building.

As it landed with a clank on the manicured grass, Lambert drew his gun.

CHAPTER TWENTY-SEVEN

The man gasped as he stared at Gabe standing in the entrance. For a moment, he was paralyzed. "You're dead," he choked out. "You sank like a stone."

"Yeah. So I guess there's no point in shooting me."

Still, Lambert raised the weapon. Before he could fire, a bolt of energy shot toward him—directed by Travis but powered by the whole group.

The thug gasped and went down. But the other two men had heard the disturbance and came running back to aid their cohort, guns drawn.

There was no time to plan, only a quick agreement that Gabe and Olivia would take the man on the right. The others took the man on the left. Two quick flashes.

The guard who had gotten the jolt from Matt and Elizabeth collapsed. But Gabe and Olivia were less successful. As their target gasped and staggered, his finger spasmed on the trigger of his automatic weapon.

But the blast kept him from shooting accurately. The bullets struck the stone walls of the building, and as they did, the group redirected their power, taking him down with a desperate blast of power.

For long moments, nobody moved. Then Gabe came cautiously out of the building, followed by Matt, Olivia, and Elizabeth.

Matt went to Lambert and checked for a pulse. "He's dead," he announced before turning to the other attackers. "Likewise."

Gabe felt a burst of triumph but also chagrin. He had endangered the whole group with his need to...kill.

He didn't like the realization. And when he felt Olivia's hand on his shoulder, he wanted to shake it off. But he stayed still.

He murdered you—twice, she reminded him.

That doesn't give me permission to go berserk.

He heard Matt laugh. *But it worked.*

I could have gotten everybody butchered.

Stop. It's done. We've evened the odds.

We don't know how many men Smith has left, but it's three fewer than he had before.

Four.

Everyone in the group stared. The new comment had come from Rachel. They all turned to see her and two more members of the road team coming over from the estate on the right.

We lost communication. What happened to you? Matt

asked. *And where are Craig and Stephanie?* His inner voice had taken on a note of alarm.

She has a flesh wound in her arm. And Craig got the top of his hair parted by a bullet. He's fine. She's okay. They were in the main line of fire from the thug who came charging out of the house. We left them in the woods across the street to make sure Smith doesn't go out the front door. Widening her reach, she asked, *Craig, can you hear us?*

Yes. We'll let you know if there's any activity out here, he added.

Why did we lose communication with you? Elizabeth asked.

Smith had some kind of mechanism to block out psychic power. It stopped us cold. We barely escaped, and we couldn't do anything until we got across the road.

Okay, so Stephanie and Craig are watching. But what's stopping him from driving away? Gabe demanded.

If he leaves, it will be on foot. None of his vehicles are currently working, Jake answered. He laughed. *Engine trouble.*

On this side of the house, there are no psychic barriers, Gabe said. *Which means we'd better be alert for traps—like the explosives he had wired to the dock.*

Right, Jake answered. *We were wondering what that big boom was. Thank God you're okay.*

We should close in on the house, Gabe said. *But use extreme caution. And spread out. We don't want the same trap catching two people.*

Olivia winced. *Or any people.*

And we're sure the surveillance equipment isn't working? Jake asked.

We're not sure of anything, Gabe shot back. *We'd better assume he can see us.*

We could cloak, the way we did when we came in for the water rescue, Rachel said. *But it takes practice. Olivia and Gabe probably can't do it.*

Goody, she muttered inwardly.

Let me clarify, Rachel said. *If his surveillance equipment isn't working, he won't know what's going on back here. He might wonder where his men are. He might wonder if we're dead. There are a lot of unknowns. But we can assume he's holed up in the house.*

Everybody looked toward the mansion, which crowned a green lawn that sloped upward from the river. They spread out and started up the slight incline toward the structure.

Gabe was getting better at telepathic communication.

Why don't you do the talking now, Travis suggested.

Ok.

That wasn't the only change he noticed. With Travis joined to him, his senses were enhanced, including a kind of awareness he couldn't exactly explain. He cast those senses ahead of them, scanning for threats. The invaders had only advanced six or seven yards when he silently shouted, *Stop. Get down on the grass.*

While everybody followed his orders, he scouted

around in a flower bed, found a rock, and threw it at a spot about ten feet farther on.

There was a jolt and a small explosion that shook the ground, followed by the appearance of a little crater where the rock had hit.

Rachel sat up and gave him an appreciative look. *How did you know?*

Travis knew. He can't tell me how.

All right, Rachel broadcast to everyone. *That's a warning to watch where you step. That's probably not the only booby trap. Gabe, take point.*

He moved to the front, and the others lined up behind him. Following his path through the minefield, they made it to the terrace. The door loomed ahead of them, but Rachel called a halt.

This is the most dangerous place. He must have the entrance fortified.

How?

I don't know. She held up a hand. *I think...After* several moments of silence, she continued. *There's only one person in the house. I think I can find him.*

How do you know he's the only one? Matt asked. *How do you know where he is?*

I can sense him. He's giving off fear vibrations big time. I can take you to him.

What about the rest of the guards?

He's the only warm body inside. We got the rest that were on duty.

How do we get in there?

Let's check the defenses. Jake picked up a heavy cast-aluminum patio chair and hurled it at the door with enough force to crash through the glass panel. Immediately, a shot rang out.

Automatic setup.

Is it safe to move forward now?

Gabe picked up another chair and threw it through the glass. Nothing happened, but that didn't prove the approach was safe.

Go in low, Matt advised. *Very low.*

He demonstrated by dropping to the concrete and belly-crawling across the threshold, where he disappeared from view. Gabe felt his stomach muscles tighten as he waited for word from inside.

Finally, Matt spoke. *I'm in a large sitting room. I'm moving to the side and staying down.*

One by one, the team belly-crawled into the house and spread out around the large room.

Is it safe to stand up? Rachel asked.

I think there's nothing else dangerous in here. Gabe cautiously stood—followed by the others.

I know where he is, Rachel said. *Before we go there, I suggest we have a plan.*

I was thinking of a way to totally disable him, Gabe answered.

Let's hear it, Jake demanded.

It could be risky

Let's hear it, Jake repeated.

They conferred in low voices for several minutes, evaluating and refining Gabe's idea.

It's dangerous for whoever takes point, Rachel said.

Yeah, that's why I'm going to do it, Gabe shot back.

I don't think you're the most effective candidate, Olivia objected.

Who is? he demanded.

If he could see Travis, it would be him. But in this case, I think it has to be me.

She was the closest to a hallway that led toward the front of the house. Gabe was still trying to formulate an objection to her plan when he saw her start to take a step.

No, he shouted in a blast that would have shattered eardrums if he'd been speaking aloud.

Leaping up, he threw her to the floor less than a second before a hail of bullets came down the hall.

He lay on top of her, his heart pounding. In the moment he'd realized the trap, terror had almost paralyzed him. But he'd pushed past it. Now he pressed her down, keeping her from getting up as Jake and Matt circled toward the doorway. Matt grabbed a lamp and threw it into the hallway. Nothing happened, but nobody was taking any chances after the near-fatal barrage.

Gabe pulled Olivia to the side, keeping her from standing as the others stayed low, moving into the hall. There were no more bursts of gunfire.

Can I sit up? Olivia asked in a shaky voice.

Yeah.

He did the same, and their eyes met.

Gabe, I...

In that moment, a wealth of emotions zinged back and forth between them, but there was no time to talk about it now. They were in the house of a man who had ordered their deaths as casually as he might have ordered a take-out pizza. And he could well have the means to do it again.

CHAPTER TWENTY-EIGHT

Harold Goddard, alias Mr. Smith, pounded the table in the control room. His anger surging, he whirled on one of the TV monitors and smashed the screen. His only accomplishment was cutting his hand. He drew it back, looking in shock at the blood welling up and running down his fingers. Shit. He'd done that to himself.

The realization increased his fury, but it also helped to ground him. He had to assume he was under attack from a group of men and women who had superhuman powers. He had to keep his cool. But what the hell was he supposed to do now? Against all odds, the invasion team had made it past the boat dock. They'd gotten into the house. They'd even defeated the psychic scrambler he'd installed out front. And before that, they'd taken out his surveillance system. Now he was Goddamn blind. He didn't know how many of them were coming. He didn't know who they were. He didn't know what had happened to any of his men.

He tried to raise Lambert on the comms system. Nothing from him or anybody else.

He'd heard gunfire somewhere outside and then from his automatic system at the patio door. But they must have gotten past it because the system in the hall had also triggered. Then nothing. And no one who had gone out had come back.

He tried once more to raise the men he'd sent to the dock. Again nothing. A while ago, he'd heard a pop from one of the land mines he'd activated on the back lawn—followed by silence.

Maybe it had gotten some of the invading deviants. But others were definitely in the house. How many? And had the hallway blast gotten them?

He spared precious moments to stick a thumb drive in the computer and download all his important files. Then he checked to make sure his Glock was in the appendix holster. It hadn't disappeared since he'd felt for it the last time.

Where were the bastards now? Should he stay here? Or try to go out the front? He pressed a hand to his temple. His mind felt muzzy, like someone was pumping nitrous oxide into the air. Sort of like he'd done at Olivia Langston's house. But that was impossible. There had been no time for anyone to set up anything like that.

With effort, he steered his jumbled thoughts back to his best tactic now. Was the safe room his best bet? If he locked himself in there, could they get to him? Or would that just be delaying capture for a few minutes?

Cautiously, he stepped out of the control room and saw —a ghost.

His eyes almost bugged out of his head as he focused on the stunning visage of Olivia Langston. But it couldn't be her. She was dead. He must be making it up. A jolt of fear stabbed him like a red-hot blade. Or was somebody making him see things that weren't there?

Ordering himself to stay calm, he studied her image. Her long auburn hair streamed back from her face as though she were the figurehead on the prow of a boat racing through the waves. Her skin was as white as marble, her white gown rippled around her legs, and she carried the scent of the sea with her as though she'd risen from the deep to come back and haunt him.

"No," he gasped.

When she said nothing, he managed, "They drowned you."

"Yes," she answered in a serene and even voice. "A very painful death it was. Think about your lungs bursting with the need for air. And when you finally have to drag in a breath, there's nothing there but water. Have you ever swallowed wrong? Of course you have. It hurts when you have to cough that little bit of liquid up. Think about how much worse it must be to drown."

He shuddered, imagining the pain of her death. Yet she was standing in front of him, talking like a living, breathing woman. Somehow, she must be making his fogged brain believe something that wasn't true. Raising his chin, he asked, "Then how are you here?"

"I came back for retribution. You almost got Matt Delano and Elizabeth Forester in the bayou. And before that, Stephanie Swift and Craig Branson. But they all got away. Some genius mastermind you are."

The slur hurt. Pressing his back against the wall, he growled, "And how would you know that?"

Instead of answering, she asked her own question. "How many people have you killed recently? Travis Carson. Gabe Bowman, me? Anybody else?"

He struggled to keep himself from shaking. The only way he could stand was to lock his legs. She couldn't be here. It was impossible. It had to be a trick. She must be alive. Which meant he could kill her.

Christ, what was he thinking—standing here talking to her? He could kill her.

With a trembling hand, he reached for the gun, but something froze his muscles. He couldn't free the weapon from the holster.

"Oh, sorry. It looks like you can't move, like when you had me strapped to that table with my hands manacled," she said. "How do you like it?"

He tried to speak, but no words came out. His chest was so tight he could hardly breathe.

"Why have you gone after the children from Dr. Solomon's experiment?" she asked.

Suddenly, the power of speech returned, but not the power to move. "Because you're dangerous," he shot back.

"You're proving it now. I was so right to keep you drugged."

"All we want is to be left alone."

"And alligators can fly."

"Where do you keep your information on the children?"

He didn't speak, but her gaze shot to his pocket. Reaching out she removed the thumb drive and closed her fist around it.

"Do you have paper records?"

He pressed his lips together. But he couldn't stop the image of the filing cabinet in his office from leaping into his mind.

"And now I know you'd like to get away from me," she soothed. "Go on. I'll give you a chance to escape my evil magic. Go out the back. If you can get down to the river, you can make your escape that way."

For a moment, he thought that was a stupid plan. Escape how? But the image fixed itself in his mind. Along with the urgent need to get away from her.

He didn't wait for her to say more. He dashed toward the back door, heading for the river. And as he ran, too late, he remembered that he'd salted the lawn with land mines —which he'd activated from the house. One had even gone off. But only one. There were a dozen more. Oh God, no. He couldn't remember where they were. He slowed down, moving more cautiously now. But he had to keep going. He had to get to the river. His escape boat was at the dock. Wait—was it? It didn't matter. He'd swim if he had to.

GABE MOVED UP BESIDE OLIVIA, who was now trembling with reaction. The illusion of her ghost costume and the wind effects were gone, and she was dressed in the dark shirt and pants she'd worn for the raid.

"Good job," he whispered.

She leaned into him, overwhelmed by her own performance.

That was Oscar-worthy.

Thanks.

From outside the house, they heard an explosion. Turning, they started toward the door, Gabe leading the way because Travis knew where the mines were planted.

They saw Smith's crumpled body. Or part of it. The leg with the foot that hit the device was missing, and blood poured from his femoral artery.

The man was moaning, gasping, crying out for help, sounding weaker by the second. Then the voice stopped, and there was only silence.

"We'd better get the records from the office, then get out of here," Rachel said. "It's only a matter of time before the police show up."

Gabe led them to the office, since Travis had explored the house while the others had been in captivity.

They grabbed the pertinent files and stuffed them into the pack Jake was carrying.

As they reached the front door, Rachel held up a hand. *The psychic scrambling...thing...could still be working.*

She heard muttered curses behind her.

Are you still there? She sent to Craig and Stephanie.

Yes. Thank God you're okay, Craig answered. *What happened? We could follow some of the action. But not all of it.*

Tell you later. Can you see or feel anything that might be projecting the anti-psychic field out there?

Yeah, we've been studying the house. I think I see something along the eaves. And something else in the shrubbery, but we didn't want to take a chance on going after them in case someone figured out what we were doing and came charging out with guns.

There's nobody left to come out. Blast them, Rachel ordered.

Craig and Stephanie did as requested, and Gabe heard a sizzling noise and smelled charred wiring.

After taking a cautious step outside, Rachel beckoned to the others, *Let's split.*

They all headed for the SUV down the road. It was a tight fit, but they managed to pile in, with Jake driving again. As they made for Route 50, they heard sirens.

Jake laughed. "A day late and a dollar short." He added, "I think we're all too tired to go very far. I made reservations at the Historic Inns of Annapolis. We can treat ourselves to some major coddling."

As they approached the bridge, Rachel said, "I know we're all on our last legs, but I need one more thing from you. Give me energy, like we did when we snuck up on the murder boat. We need to disable the camera and plate reader at the toll booth so nobody knows we were here."

They all joined in the stealth operation, erasing any evidence that they had been on the Eastern Shore.

Completely wiped out, Olivia dozed off on the way to Annapolis. She opened her eyes as they pulled up at the hotel complex. But she was still on the wrong side of coherent.

Jake went in and registered for the group, collecting room keys. The complex had several buildings. Gabe grabbed his and Olivia's bags and led her along State Circle toward an imposing red brick building with a high-pitched roof sporting several dormer windows. As they made their way along the brick sidewalk, she found herself waking up to the reality of what came next. The closer they got to the entrance, the more her stomach knotted and her nerve endings sizzled. She stole a quick glance at Gabe, but his gaze was fixed on the looming building, and his thoughts were sealed away from her.

After he unlocked the front door, she followed him down a short hall to their room. It turned out to be a small suite decorated in colonial style with dark wood furniture and formal draperies. Beyond the parlor was a bedroom with a king-sized bed and a luxury modernized bathroom.

Gabe focused on the king-sized bed. "You probably need to sleep," he said. "I can take the sofa out here."

"No," she said, closing the distance between them and grasping his arm. Her touch made him jump, then turn slowly to face her. She lifted her chin so that she could meet his eyes.

"I'm not going to push you into anything," he continued. "I know you need time to adjust to…" He stopped and shrugged. "If you *can* adjust," he added, his tone barely audible.

"Don't," she said.

"Don't what?"

"Put up barriers between us."

He kept his tone even. "I'm not…the man you fell in love with."

"Yes, you still are, and a lot more."

When he stayed where he was, she took a step toward him, knowing she had to be the one to prove the point. When she was only inches away, she reached for him, wrapping her arms around him, pulling him close, reveling in the feel of his solid masculine body. When she had gotten close to Travis, she had longed for this kind of physical contact. Now she had it.

He stood for long moments, as though he were simply enduring her attentions. Then his arms came up to embrace her, and she let out the breath she'd been holding.

"Thank you," she breathed.

He cleared his throat. "Before we go any further…*if* we go any further, you need to know what you're getting into."

She answered with a small nod.

His next words were not spoken aloud. *I'm Gabe Bowman. I have all his memories, all his skills, and all his aspirations. But I'm also Travis Carson. I have his memories and his skills.* He swallowed. *And his needs and desires. He found you when he was lost. You brought him back to life, and you bonded like the other couples who were children of the Solomon clinic. You're still bonded. Only Gabe Bowman is part of that equation now.*

Stop talking about yourself in the third person. I found out who you are in no uncertain terms when we went back to Smith's estate to make sure he couldn't do to anyone else what he'd done to us.

As she felt some of the tension ease out of him, she tightened her hold. *I don't have any doubts about what I want and what I need...from you.*

At the same time, her hands began to slide up and down his back, pulling him close.

He lowered his head. She raised hers, and their mouths came together with a mutual expression of need.

His lips moved against hers, caressing and questing. She was doing the same, reveling in all the sensations she had craved.

He didn't have to speak for her to know what he was thinking. They had been in a rather messy battle, and they would turn any bed into a pigsty now.

The shower.

Their mouths broke apart so they could watch where they were going, but they didn't turn each other loose. Together, they stumbled into the bathroom, which thankfully had a large walk-in shower. He reached behind her to turn on the hot water, fumbling to adjust it as she began to pull off his clothing. She dispatched his shirt and started on his zipper while he did the same for her, both frantic to shed what had become encumbrances.

They left a pile of muddy, grass-stained clothing on the floor as they stepped under the spray, clinging together because they needed the stability. His hands moved everywhere they could reach, over her arms, across her shoulders, down her back to the swell of her butt, raising a firestorm everywhere they touched. She was doing the same, reveling in the feel of his slick skin under her fingertips.

He tilted her away from himself so that he could lower his head to find her breasts with his mouth, licking and sucking and bringing her nipples to hard points of sensation.

She wanted to wrap her fingers around his penis, but he warned her against it, silently telling her that he wanted this to last.

He might want that, but she knew it was an impossible goal. They were both too needy, too greedy to postpone fulfillment for long. He leaned back against the wall, lifting her up so that he could slide into her. There was no fumbling, no call for her to help him find the right place. He *knew*. And he knew exactly what she needed to reach climax.

He moved her body forward and away, the rhythm quickly growing frantic. She knew he was judging her reactions, following her progress toward completion. When her inner muscles began to contract, she felt him let go, both of them exploding in a burst of satisfaction that took them to the moon and back.

She collapsed against him, still hardly able to believe that they had just done this together. Her body responded to his, and he gave back everything he took.

When he eased her down, they clung together under the spray, swaying slightly, trying to take it in.

In the afterglow, she sensed Travis with her the way he had been with her before everything had changed. And she knew they had lost nothing, only gained more than she could ever have imagined.

As the water sluiced over them, she let herself open to his thoughts. He had been two different men who had somehow merged into one—were still merging in ways they were still exploring.

There won't be hot water left for anyone else in the hotel, she finally whispered in his mind. *Maybe we'd better use the shower for its primary purpose.*

The suggestion led to hands slick with soap and bodies that heated again, never mind the water temperature. This time, they had more restraint. They washed each other, dried each other, and stepped out of the shower ready for round two.

Sorry. I have to dry my hair, or we'll get the pillows wet.

Not a problem.

She watched him watching her, his expression greedy as she did a quick and dirty job on her long, thick mane. When it was almost dry, they staggered across the bedroom together and climbed under the covers, rocking in each other's arms before making love again. This time it was slow and delicious rather than frantic.

She felt his smile as his mouth traveled down her body, finding her center and teasing her until she was begging for release.

But not this way, I want you inside me again.

He wrapped her in his arms, and at the same time, she felt his hands in places on her body he shouldn't be able to reach.

How are you doing?

Don't know. But I like it.

Me too.

Words became impossible as they climbed together above the earth's atmosphere, then streaking back like a meteor to land in this lovely, comfortable bed.

The miracle of Travis bringing Gabe back would never be lost on either of them.

As they lay tangled together, she tried to absorb the reality of the man who held her close. It was still a wonderment.

For me too. But the thing I know best is that I love you.

She knitted her fingers with his. He could read her thoughts. She didn't have to say that she loved Travis. And she felt the joy of having Gabe, too. The totality of what she had with this man was just beginning.

She read his silent response, all his feelings open to her. She waited a beat before asking, *You're sure you want me to call you Gabe?*

He laughed softly. *That's an easy decision. All the people in my life already know me as Gabe.*

Are we going to join the others in...Lafayette?

Decorah Security has a New Orleans office, but what about your business? You have a reputation here.

I think I can build one in Louisiana. I want to be with the rest of the group, at least for a while. They saved us. We wouldn't be here without them.

And they wouldn't be free of the threat of Mr. Smith hanging over them—without us.

Yes. But I need to stop in at my office and tell Frank what happened.

Will he believe you?

Frank...yeah. He collects agents with talents you couldn't imagine.

Like what?

He hesitated for a moment, and she knew the answer to the question wasn't something he spoke of with outsiders.

I'm not an outsider.

Right. Okay, like, the Marshall cousins are all werewolves.

She might have thought he was joking, but she knew from his thoughts that it was true.

I'll fit right in. He made a dismissive sound. *In fact, I used to feel jealous of their powers. Wait till they see what I've got.*

She laughed, liking the sound and the new sense of

freedom enveloping her. They had gone through hell in the past few days, but they had come out together, and she knew the future would be glorious.

"Something else we have to take care of," he said aloud.

She caught the thought in his mind.

"Your aunt. She hired Gabe to find out what happened to Travis." She paused for a moment. "Does she give any credence to the paranormal? Would she believe..." She lifted one shoulder. "That you were dead, but you found me and held on, and then Gabe gave you a body again?"

"She'd probably think I was trying to get out of admitting failure at not saving him."

The scene when Gabe interviewed the feisty old woman made her shake her head. But she wasn't going to give up on the idea. "What if you told her something that Gabe Bowman couldn't possibly know?"

"That might work."

"Is the guy who rented Jake the boat going to remember him?"

"I don't think so."

"It's gonna be hard to explain how it ended up in pieces at Smith's estate."

"Maybe one of the others will have some ideas about that."

"Or it's gonna be the St. Stephens mystery of the century."

They talked for a few more minutes, warm and cozy in bed. But they were both too tired to keep their eyes open.

As Olivia drifted off, she found Gabe's hand again, secure in the knowledge that he would be there when she woke beside him.

ALSO BY REBECCA YORK

SCIENCE FICTION ROMANCE

Off-World Series

Hero's Welcome (an off-world series short story)

Nightfall (an off-world series novella)

Conquest (an off-world series short story)

Assignment Danger (an off-world novella)

Christmas Home (an off-world short story)

Firelight Confession (an off-world novella)

Escape Velocity

PARANORMAL ROMANTIC SUSPENSE

Decorah Security Series

On Edge (a Decorah Security prequel novella)

Dark Moon (a novel)

Dark Powers (a novel)

Rx Missing (a novel)

Found Missing (a novel)

Hunter (a novel)

Trapped (a novel)

Scene of the Crime (a novel)

Hollow Moon (a novella)

Fire on the Moon (a novel)

Terror Mansion (a novella)

At Risk

Hunting Moon

Preying Game

Cursed

Man From Nowhere

Christmas Captive

Soulmated Series

Sudden Insight

Sudden Attraction

Overwhelming Attraction

Diagnosis Attraction

Midnight Obsession

ABOUT THE AUTHOR

A New York Times and USA Today Best-Selling Author, Rebecca York is a 2011 recipient of the Romance Writers of America Centennial Award. Her career has focused on romantic suspense, often with paranormal elements.

Her 16 Berkley books and novellas include her nine-book werewolf "Moon" series. KILLING MOON was a launch book for the Berkley Sensation imprint. She has written over 50 books for Harlequin Intrigue, many in her popular 43 Light Street series.

She has written for Harlequin, Berkley, Dell, Tor, Carina Press, Silhouette, Kensington, Running Press, Tudor, Pageant Books, Scholastic, and Sourcebooks.

Her many awards include two Rita finalist books. She has two Career Achievement awards from Romantic Times: for Series Romantic Suspense and for Series Romantic Mystery. And her Peregrine Connection series won a Lifetime Achievement Award for Romantic Suspense Series.

Many of her novels have been nominated for or won RT Reviewers Choice awards. In addition, she has won a Prism Award, several New Jersey Romance Writers Golden Leaf awards and numerous other chapter awards.

Oliver Heber Books is now publishing her Decorah Security Series, her Off World Series, and her Soulmated Series.

OLIVERHEBERBOOKS

A small press bound by the belief that every voice matters.

Sign up for our newsletter to learn about new releases and more.
https://oliver-heberbooks.com/subscribe/

Follow us on social media:

facebook.com/oliverheberbooks

instagram.com/oliverheberbooks

amazon.com/oliverheberbooks

youtube.com/@OliverHeberBooksPublisher